Shelby's Secret

Poison Pen, Volume 6

Marissa Ann and Rae Goldman

Published by Marissa Ann, 2023.

This is a work of fiction. Similarities to real people, places, or events are entirely coincidental.

SHELBY'S SECRET

First edition. July 7, 2023.

Copyright © 2023 Marissa Ann and Rae Goldman.

ISBN: 979-8223299783

Written by Marissa Ann and Rae Goldman.

Table of Contents

Prologue

Shelby

I scratch on the pad in front of me with the pen my lawyer, Taylor, gave to me, not really writing anything.

He knows me well enough by now to realize I need a distraction so that my eyes don't wander over to my ex-husband, Greyson.

His eyes have burned a hole into the side of my head just as they've done for the past week we've had to be in this courtroom.

The judge is currently in another room so that he can talk to the children in private. I was thankful for that, not wanting them to have to face their own father in these circumstances.

Out of the corner of my eye, I see Grey once again look this way. His knee started bouncing about thirty minutes ago with impatience.

I recognize it for what it is. He's scared now of what the outcome will be.

When all of this first started, he came in every day with a small smirk on his face as if he knew he had already won.

Taylor had a serious time calming my fears that I had already lost. He has assured me more than once that everything will work out the way that it should.

I still have my doubts though.

"All rise!"

Taylor helps me to my feet as my eyes look to the door the judge will be coming back through. I can hear my own heartbeat in my ears and I must sway a little as Taylor grips my arm a little firmer to get my attention.

"Just breathe." He whispers, staring straight into my eyes and I do as he says.

He doesn't break eye contact until he assures himself that I'm not about to pass out on the floor.

"You may be seated." The judge announces, shuffling the papers on his desk. He's quiet for so long that I begin to shake again.

"Do the two counselor's have anything further to add before I announce my decision?" He asks, looking at Taylor first.

"No your Honor. I feel confident that we have presented all the facts in this case." Taylor answers.

"Thank you, Counselor Burns. What about the defendant? Do you or your client have anything further to add?" He looks over to Grey and his entire set of lawyers.

I make the mistake of looking over there as well and lock eyes with Grey. His lip curls up slightly while his eyes shoot daggers.

My heart starts to race again and I feel as though I'm about to have another panic attack.

Just as I begin to lose air in my lungs, I feel someone squeeze my hand and I glance down to look at Taylor's hand. He squeezes reassuringly as I glance up to look at him.

Feeling slightly better, I look to the judge who surprisingly is looking right at me and I wonder what I missed Grey's attorney's saying about me.

"Well if that is all, I have made my decision." He says, looking between all of us. "In the matter of Divorce; I grant Shelby Lynn Porter the right to divorce from her husband, Greyson Porter. She is also granted the right to take back her maiden name if she so wishes." I can't stop the grin from forming on my own face.

"In the interest of the minor children; two year old Dyna Porter and five year old Bryson Porter, I hereby grant Full Physical and Legal custody to their Mother, Shelby Lynn Nicholson Porter.

Mrs. Nicholson Porter has waived all rights to child support at this time. I will agree with that. As for visitation for Mr. Porter with the minor children. At this time, I will not grant any."

"What?" Greyson yells before his attorneys can stop him.

"Mr. Porter, I order you to take anger management as well as counseling. In six months, you can reapply to the court for visitation."

"You fucking bitch!" Greyson screams.

Everything becomes a blur then as he somehow makes it over to my side of the room without anyone stopping him.

My lungs are screaming for air and it takes my brain several long seconds to realize his hands are around my throat squeezing as hard as he can.

I can't hear anything as my vision begins to go black. I'm finally free of him, only to die by his hand.

Please, God, watch over my babies. It's the last thought I have before I pass out.

I wake up later in the hospital with them doing all kinds of tests to make sure my neck and everything is okay. Taylor seems to be way more frantic than I currently am which is a little insane.

"You can't stay around here. Sure he's in jail at the moment but you know it's only a matter of time before he makes bail." Taylor argues from across the hospital room.

"We have nowhere else to go." My voice is barely above a whisper.

Reaching up, I barely rub my neck where Greyson's hands had been.

I'm beyond sure there would have been if they hadn't been able to pull him off of me.

"Arin and I have a suggestion about that. If you're willing to listen to it." He turns, looking right at me.

"What is it?" I ask just as the nurses come in with my discharge paperwork.

"We'll talk about it in the car. Let's just get you out of here and go pick up your kids." He smiles softly, knowing exactly how to distract me.

"They're probably wondering where I'm at. I promised them I'd be there to get them before bedtime." I raise up, signing the papers the nurse hands me.

"But, seriously, what's the suggestion?" I ask as he wheels me out of the room in a wheelchair.

"Well...It's not really a suggestion. It's more of a demand from Arin."

I look up at him, knowing this should be really good. I've known him and his wife long enough now to know that when Arin wants something, she will get it. One way or another.

Chapter 1

Shelby

I watch out the window of the private plane I'm in as it circles the airport, waiting for a runway.

I'm still trying to pinpoint when everything went wrong. Was I a bad wife? A bad mom? Did I deserve to be treated the way my now ex-husband treated me?

Bryson, my five year old son, has barely said a word since his father broke his arm. I thank God every day that Dyna is too young to know what's happening at only three years old.

My parents never liked Grey, they said he was too old for me. After the cruise ship they were on sank, I wanted nothing more than to hide away.

Grey wouldn't let me. He practically had to drag me out of the house, not allowing me to wallow in depression.

Six months after their deaths, I was married. Looking back it's like I was surrounded by fog. Everything is blurry and moving faster than the speed of light.

Then six months later I was pregnant with Bry. His birth brought me back to reality. Named after my dad, he gave me a reason to live.

The first time Grey hit me, Bry was around three months old. He had been colicky and crying. I was at my wits end and made the mistake of asking my husband for help. The slap came out of nowhere.

"Grey, help me please," I begged.

"What do you expect me to do at two in the morning?" He demanded.

"Please Grey, I haven't slept in three days."

That's when it happened. I was so shocked by the sting in my cheek, I was speechless. After that, it was a slap here, a pinch there. Nothing I did was right.

I became a recluse, almost never leaving the house. I couldn't risk anyone seeing the bruises. Ashamed they would think like my husband, that I was a bad wife, a bad mom, and deserved to be smacked around.

Homeschooled to hide me from paparazzi, orphaned then married at eighteen, a mom at nineteen, I was so sheltered and naive.

The thought of my husband messing with my birth control and me becoming pregnant again two years after Bryson was born never crossed my mind.

Dyna was a blessing in more than one way. Grey didn't hurt me as often because he knew with all my medical appointments, someone might see or suspect something. He acted like a doting husband for exactly nine months.

However, it didn't take long for him to flip the switch after her birth. I had to reschedule my six-week follow-up three times because of bruised ribs.

"Shut that brat up!" He screamed at me the first time she cried during the night.

I got her fed and back to sleep but when I tried climbing into bed, he raised his foot and kicked me in the ribs, sending me flying across the room.

"Go sleep somewhere else! I have an important meeting in the morning." He yelled.

The final straw was when he came home early one day. I was feeding Bry and Dyna. Dyna was making a mess out of her dinner as usual and Bry was playing with his food. There was nothing unusual about it all, dinner was always a frustrating event with two kids under five.

Grey walked in, looked around at the mayhem, and lost it. He grabbed Bryson's arm dragging him from the table and threw him into his room, then came back and proceeded to yell about what a crap mom I am for letting the kids get out of control.

He left me curled in a ball on the kitchen floor, scooping Dyna out of her high chair on his way out of the room.

"Come on Little Princess." He cooed at her. "Mommy needs to clean up this mess."

The only good thing I can say about Greyson Porter is that he loves his daughter.

I was still cleaning the kitchen when Bryson poked his head around the corner.

"Mommy my arm hurts." He whimpered.

"Oh My God!" I gasped when I saw his little arm swollen and blue.

I managed to hold it together through the emergency room visit and questioning from the medical staff.

Grey told the doctor that he had been playing, wrestling with his son when the injury occurred. He was always good at conning people into believing him.

I stayed quiet not contradicting his version of events, but in my head, I was already planning our escape. After Grey left for work the next day, I packed up the kids and went to a women's shelter.

We hid at the shelter for almost three months before I got the courage to file for divorce. One of the other residents gave me a number for Taylor Burns.

When I first contacted him, I didn't realize he was in Alaska but he assured me that he often worked cases in California and it wasn't a big deal.

The first time we met in person he brought his wife Arin with him. We became instant friends, exchanging phone numbers before they left.

"Shelby, Shelby?" Taylor's voice pulls me from the memories.

"We've landed," He tells me.

Gathering up Bryson and Dyna, we leave the plane. Once we clear the steps, I'm pulled into an awkward hug.

I jump and start to pull away until I realize it's Arin. With Dyna squished between us, I start crying.

"None of that now," She commands and I start laughing.

Arin is bossy and outgoing, the complete opposite of me. I've never had a friend like her who honestly cares about me, not like the ones I left behind that refused to speak to me after I left Grey.

We have nothing except the clothes on our backs since I can't access my trust fund until I turn thirty.

I couldn't even pay Taylor but he still agreed to represent me. Now they are offering me a job and protection.

Marrying Greyson was the worst thing to ever happen to me but getting divorced is the best because it brought Arin and Taylor into my life.

After Greyson lost control in the courtroom, the first thing Taylor did was call his wife. There was no hesitation, Arin demanded he bring us home.

I was unsure at first without a way to pay for basic necessities but then Arin proposed I work for her.

Their babysitter was leaving and in exchange for watching the kids while they worked I would have an apartment just for us.

When Arin steps back from our hug she notices the bruises on my throat and traces them with her fingers.

"I have friends," she whispers so that Taylor can't hear her words. "You say the word and that man won't ever touch another woman."

Maybe I should be scared about how serious she is, but instead, I start laughing.

I'm laughing so hard that I have to put Dyna down so I don't drop her. There are still tears streaming down my face but they aren't sad tears anymore and I think that was Arin's goal.

After taking a minute to pull myself together, I realize Arin isn't alone. She introduces me to the two women standing behind her.

"Shelby, these are my co-workers and friends, Cassandra and Mika. Mika is Taylor's sister and you've met her husband Atka, Taylor's partner. Cassandra's husband Jake, owns the gym where you'll be joining us in self-defense class."

"It's nice to finally meet you," I tell them awkwardly, holding my hand out to shake. "I've heard a lot about you."

"I bet you have." Mika laughs, ignoring my hand and pulling me in for a hug. It's not easy with her very pregnant belly in the middle but she manages it.

Once she steps back, a tug on my pants leg gets my attention. Looking down I see that Bryson is holding one of his sister's hands, with the other one she is reaching for me.

"I hungry, Mama" Dyna tells me.

That's when Cass steps up, "Come on. The guys can run her stuff over to the apartment while we take the little ones out for something to eat."

"Good idea," Arin agrees. "We can swing by Mama Lou's and pick up Aiden, Livy and Liza then take them all over to Stella's place." She turns back to me and continues, "Stella's is a little restaurant close to the shop that has an indoor playground. It'll give you all a chance to meet the kids."

"Shouldn't I help the guys?" I ask, hesitating.

"Nah," Arin waves them off. "They got it."

"Well then, that sounds great. They've been cooped up on the plane for a few hours. If they don't run off some steam they'll be up all night." I agree.

Before I know it, we are climbing into the back of a passenger van and the kids are buckled in car seats.

"The van is rented for the day so we can all ride together but the car seats are yours to keep," Arin explains as she climbs in the driver's seat.

"You need a ladder there?" Taylor calls across the parking lot.

"Nope," Arin calls back. "Just wait until the kids are in bed tonight and I'll climb you like a ladder."

I'm used to the way they tease and play so I pretend I didn't hear a thing. "Oh, thank goodness. Car seats honestly never crossed my mind. Taylor said everything was within walking distance." I say as I buckle my seatbelt.

Fifteen minutes later we pull up in front of a building that has a big sign on the front. It says Mama Lou's daycare. On the door is a smaller sign that reads: Closing soon. Mika sits with me while Cass and Arin go in for their kids.

It takes longer to get the kids loaded and buckled in than it did to get here from the airport but we are soon on our way again.

Only two blocks away from the daycare, Mika points out Poison Pen. "There is the shop and the apartment you'll be living in is right above it. The park is another block this way, in walking distance if you want to take the kids out on nice days and Arin's house is just a few blocks away."

"Stella's, the place we're going to eat is another couple of blocks from the park. They have an indoor play area for cold and rainy days. Also in walking distance are a grocery store, the gym Cass' husband owns and a couple of bars but I don't imagine you'll be hanging out at them." Arin picks up where Mika left off then Cass jumps in.

"Mika and Atka have been spending time out at the tribal village, but they are having a house built near Arin's. Jake and I live out in the sticks though. My husband likes his privacy."

Arin starts laughing and nudges Cass in the ribs, "You like it as much as he does. Don't pretend you don't jump on Jake under the stars every chance you get."

"Mama, why would Aunty Cass jump on Uncle Jake? Don't do that Aunty Cass, I don't want Uncle Jake to get hurt!" A stern little girl voices from the backseat.

There is a moment of complete silence in the van before we all burst out laughing.

The van is barely parked when Cass jumps out and runs around to the back door. "Olivia baby, I would never hurt Uncle Jake, you know that right?"

"But Mama said ..." Olivia answers.

"Mama was only teasing me," Cass tells her.

"Mama! It's not nice to tease our friends. Mama Lou said so!"

I turn away so Olivia can't see me laughing and notice Mika doing the same thing. I suspect this girl is going to be just like her mom when she grows up.

"You're right," Arin tells her. "I'm sorry for teasing you Cass."

Her words sound sincere but the laughter in her eyes is shining through as we unload the kids.

Mika must be a mind reader because as we walk into the restaurant she slides up next to me and says, "It's hereditary, wait until you meet Naomi, her older daughter. She'll be here in a couple of weeks for the picnic."

It takes me a moment but then I remember her mentioning the daughter she had to give up for adoption when she was fifteen. Naomi lives in Montana with her adoptive mom but they are all close.

Once we enter the restaurant, Mika claims a table while Arin, Cass, and I get the kids set up. Before we even order our food, Olivia is begging to play. Arin puts her food down and tells the kids they have to eat first.

Bryson and Dyna are unusually quiet but they are probably even more overwhelmed than I am. They don't understand why we left everything behind and they have never been around so many new people.

We've barely gotten settled at the table when our server arrives. She is quick and efficient, before I know it everyone is eating. I think I'm going to like this place.

Once the kids eat they run off to play, even little Liza toddles over to the ball pit.

"Are you sure you want to do this?" Arin asks me. "These kids are a lot of work. It will mostly be Olivia and Aiden but once in a while, Cass will need you to keep Liza. We'll start you off slowly because Mama Lou has a few weeks before she leaves and we want the kids to get comfortable with you."

"I have to. I owe you and Taylor so much." I tell her.

"No, you don't!" Arin interrupts me. "All of us," she says pointing to each woman at the table, "Came from shitty situations. We would do this for you even if you never spend a minute of time with our kids. That apartment is yours as long as you need it."

Taking a deep breath to prevent tears from spilling down my face, I tell her "I don't know how to do anything except take care of kids. My parents kept me locked away from everything for most of my life. The paparazzi would have paid millions for just one picture of me.

The only people I ever came in contact with were the household staff and some of their business associates, Grey was one of them. He swept me off my feet because I so desperately wanted human contact. I didn't even know until a year after my parents died that they had fired him. By then it was too late, I was married to him and expecting Bry."

Reaching over and squeezing my hand, Cass says "We can fix that." I must have a weird look on my face because she goes on to explain, "You won't have the kids 24/7. You could take classes online. The University of Anchorage has enrollment options."

"But how would I pay for that?" I can't help but ask. "I'll get a monthly allowance from my trust fund, but I need that for Bry and Dyna. There is no way I would qualify for financial aid."

"We'll help," Mika says.

"But I couldn't accept that. You all are already doing so much for me."

"The first time Arin came home after meeting you, she told me, I have a new sister. You are family now and family helps each other. We'll do this for you now and one day we might need your help." Mika states.

"Besides," Cass interrupts. "I'm not sure if you know it but the three of us," She makes a circle with her hand around the table. "We don't have to work. We choose to work, helping you won't hurt any of us financially or otherwise."

With tears streaming freely down my face, I don't know how to respond to this conversation. I'm almost grateful it ends when a cry from the play area has all of us jumping to see which kid is crying and why.

We find Liza at the top of the slide crying. Not wanting to be left out she had followed the bigger kids through the tunnel and was too scared to go down the slide. Without a thought,

I climb the ladder and crawl through the tunnel to get to her. Pulling her onto my lap, we slide down together to meet Cass at the bottom.

Pulling Liza into her arms, she tells me "This is why you're perfect for the job. I couldn't have climbed through that tunnel. My husband was kidnapped and stashed in the crawlspace under a house. I haven't been able to go into small spaces since I pulled him out. Thank you."

"Wow, What?" I look to her for more information but Arin steps up and suggests we get the kids settled in.

Once everyone is loaded up with Arin back behind the wheel, she drops off Cass and Liza first since they are the farthest out. Then swings by her house to drop off Mika, Olivia and Aiden. Finally pulling into the alley behind Poison Pen she leads me and my kids upstairs to our new home.

Chapter 2

Shelby

"Come on you two, it's time to go pick up Olivia and Aiden from daycare."

Dyna squeals with delight, skipping to the front door as best she can on her little legs.

Bryson, being a more quiet kid by nature, walks at a slower pace towards us.

"Are we still going to the park mama?" Bry asks, smiling up at me as I grab my purse.

"Absolutely kiddo." I grin down at him, reaching out to gently push his hair back away from his eyes.

Bryson grabs his sister's hand, leading her out of the door. He's always been an amazing big brother, trying to keep his sister out of trouble.

Sometimes I wonder if his nature was always supposed to be this way. Quiet, more reserved. Or was he made to be this way after living around his father for so long.

My mind has been wondering lots of things since we got here almost a week ago. There's times where I wish I could go back and never marry Greyson but then if I hadn't, I wouldn't have my sweet kids.

I should have left after Dyna was born. Maybe then, Bryson would have been young enough to learn to be a kid. Loud, rambunctious and learned that getting dirty wasn't a bad thing. Hopefully, it's not too late for him to still have all of that.

"Mama?" Bryson's voice pulls me back to the present.

Looking up, I see that we are standing in front of Mama Lou's daycare. Glancing back at Bry, I shake my head. My boy is a wonder. I don't think I know any child that at the age of five, almost six as he likes to remind me, that would remember the way back to a place he's been to only a few times.

Walking inside, the kids follow behind me. It's louder here with so many kids running and playing.

"Shelby! How are you today?" Mama Lou asks, walking up to the counter.

"Pretty good actually. I promised the kids I'd take them to the park to play for a while." I smile at the sweet woman I met the first day we arrived.

"Oh, well, that should be a lot of fun!" She smiles down at Dyna who giggles back.

Another teacher walks Aiden and Olivia up to the front, handing me their backpacks.

"It was good seeing you." I say to Mama Lou, turning the kids back to the door.

"Wait. I have something that would be useful for you. Besides, with this place closing down, I'd have to throw it out anyway." Mama Lou, rushes through a door.

I look over at the other teacher who smiles, shrugging her shoulders. A few minutes later, Mama Lou comes back pushing what looks like a giant stroller that is currently folded up.

"What is it?" I ask, my brows drawing together.

"It's a group stroller. This thing is awesome and it's not super heavy. Come outside, I'll show you how to open it up. This way, when these four are all tuckered out from playing at the playground, you'll have an easier time getting them back home."

Outside on the sidewalk, I watch as she unfolds it and starts helping the kids into the seats, buckling them in.

"Thank you so much. I'll bring it back tomorrow when I pick the kids up."

"No ma'am. I'm giving this to you. As I said, I'd have to throw it out anyway." She puts her hands on her hips.

"Well, at least let me pay for it." I offer, not wanting to take it for nothing.

"Absolutely not. I'm giving it to you. You can use it. When the kids outgrow it or you don't need it any more, give it away to someone else." She smiles.

"Thank you Mama Lou. I appreciate it." I smile back.

"No problem. See you tomorrow!" She waves, turning to go back inside.

Looking back at the kids, all four strapped into the giant stroller, they all grin back at me.

"You four ready to go?"

"Yep!" They all yell at the same time. Shaking my head, I grin widely as we all make our way to the park.

An hour later, I'm sitting on a bench watching the kids play as I look to see if my monthly allowance from my trust fund has been posted yet.

Olivia and Bryson are currently building what appears to be a huge sand castle in the sand box. Aiden and Dyna are on the toddler swings.

At first they wanted me to push them both but now they are determined to swing on their own. They are low enough to the ground the kids feet touch but watching them try to coordinate their little legs to do as they are supposed to has me hiding my giggles behind my hand.

Hearing a roar coming from the road, I look in that direction and see several motorcycles as they begin to pass.

Looking back at the kids, I see Olivia look in that direction as well and grin widely. She must love motorcycles or something with the way she is staring at them.

Looking back down at my screen, I'm disappointed to see that it has yet to post. Thinking about calling my parents' estate lawyer, I don't hear the footsteps coming up from behind me but I definitely hear the booming voice when he pretty much yells almost right in my ear.

"Who the fuck are you?" He demands.

I jump slightly from his tone and quickly turn around, narrowing my eyes.

"Excuse me? Who are you to even ask?" My fists ball into a tight knot.

"I want to know who the fuck you are and what you're doing with Arin's kids?" His nostrils flare and his eyes slowly look at me from head to toe. I shiver slightly and don't understand if it's from fright or the slighter cooler temperature that is Alaska.

"Uncle Glitch!" Olivia yells, running right into the man's legs.

He looks down and his face completely transforms with the smile he gives to her.

"Hey, Pumpkin. What have you been up to today?" He asks her.

As she proceeds to tell him all about what she did at daycare, I take my time looking at him. Olivia obviously knows this man. She called him Uncle Glitch. Having not noticed before, I realize just how handsome he is. Especially when he smiles.

"Aunt Shelby bwought us to the park. Bwy helping to make a castle for a pwincess to live in. Wanta see?"

"I sure do. You go ahead, I'll be right there." He smiles, putting her back onto her feet and she scampers off.

"Aunt Shelby, huh? You Arin's sister or something?" He asks in a much calmer voice.

"Or something." I raise my brow, giving him nothing.

He looks at me far longer than he should before giving me a grin that probably melts panties.

"You're something, alright." He turns towards the kids and heads in their direction.

I watch for several long seconds to see how well Bry takes a stranger coming to sit by him. He looks at the man as he talks to him. I'm not sure what he says but Bryson smiles a smile I've not seen from him in a really long time.

Grabbing my phone from the seat, I dial Arin's number and hope she's not in the middle of working on a tattoo.

"Hey, everything okay?" Her voice comes over the line.

"Who is Glitch?" I blurt out in a hushed whisper.

"Um, why? Is everything okay?" Her voice gets a little frantic.

"The kids are fine. He showed up here at the park demanding to know who I was, like I was some kidnapper or something." My heart beats quickly now that it's all over.

"He's harmless. He's in Atka's brother's motorcycle club. Sort of. The kids love him. Well they love all the guys really and the guys love them. I'm sorry if he scared you. I'll call him."

"No. There's no need. Really. We are all fine, really. He didn't so much as scare me as he surprised me."

Getting a feeling that someone is watching me, I look back at the sandbox and see that Glitch has his eyes right on me. I can't decipher the look that's on his face though.

"Are you sure?" Arin asks.

"He's not a crazy lunatic, is he?" I ask, not breaking eye contact with Glitch on the other side of the park.

Arin laughs at my question. "He's not a lunatic. I'm going to call him anyway. Tell him he better leave you alone or I'll kick his ass."

I laugh, shaking my head. "Sorry I bothered you at work."

"Hey, there's no reason for you to be sorry. Dinner is at my house this evening after our class. Taylor is cooking!"

"Do I need to bring anything?" I ask.

"Nope. He has everything covered. I'll see you later."

After we hang up, I sit back on the bench where I was before Glitch interrupted me.

What kind of name is that anyway? Surely his parents didn't name him that. Imagining him as a kid with that name, he probably got into a lot of fights over it. I giggle to myself thinking about it.

Hearing a phone ring, I look up to see Glitch answer his own. His eyes shoot directly to me and I know that it's Arin on the other end. His eyes hold mine for several long moments before I jerk mine away. That's when I notice how fast my heart is racing yet again.

Glitch

"Hey man, where the fuck you run off to? We looked behind us and you were gone." Sticks asks as I take a seat at the bar.

"I stopped at the park to play with Arin and Taylor's kids." I shrug, purposely not mentioning my real reasons for stopping.

"The Prez says they got a new sitter from the lower forty eight. We're supposed to keep our eye on her."

"Oh yeah? There a reason why? She in trouble or something?" I ask, truly curious now to know more about her.

Maybe I should just look into her myself.

"Or something. I'm sure he'll fill everyone in at Church this evening."

Turning to look at him, I study him carefully. He looks exactly like his old man although he doesn't even realize it. Hell, he doesn't even know who his real father is.

"Sticks, how is it you always know what's going on before the Prez even tells us?" I ask.

"It's his ears, man. I'm telling you, musically inclined people can hear everything!" Mac comments as he walks over to us.

"You're so full of shit." I shake my head.

"That's why he wears a skirt. Makes it easier to go to the shitter!" Sticks laughs.

"It's a bloody kilt! You assholes!" Mac slams his fist on the bar, turning to stomp away.

"Going to shit again?" Sticks yells at his back and Mac flips him off as he walks away.

"Why do you rile him up?" I chuckle.

"Because it's fun. Have you ever watched how he blushes like a girl any time you call it a skirt?"

"That's not a blush, it's anger and one of these days he's going to hang you by the balls from the rafters." I say.

"He'd have to catch me first." Sticks shrugs.

We both jump a little as a quiet voice behind us says, "You should learn a little respect."

"Fucking hell, Spector. Don't sneak up on people!" I turn to glare at him.

"I didn't sneak. You two bone heads are just hard of hearing." Spector comments before he turns to leave just as quietly as he came.

"Jesus. If anyone in this club fucking scares me, it's him." Sticks nods towards Spector's back.

Looking in that direction, Spector seems to go still for only a second as if he heard Sticks before he starts walking again.

These two have history and until Spector is ready to tell the truth about the past, there will always be a distance between them.

Shelby

"Hey, there you are!" Cass says as I walk into the building.

"Wow. This place is huge! I didn't think there would be that big of a market for a workout center up here." I look around at all the equipment and people working on.

"Well, there are locals who like it so they don't have to contend with all the bugs outside but a lot of the doctors send patients here for certain types of rehab. The bonus is the self-defense classes Jake offers. The women really love it. For more than just the benefits of knowing how to help yourself, I'm sure." She laughs as we watch a woman fawn over Jake.

He looks back at Cass with a look that clearly says, Save Me but she continues to watch with her own little smirk on her face.

"Are you not going to help the poor guy?" Mika asks, seeing it all as well.

"Hell no. It's too fun to watch." We all laugh as Cass refuses to budge.

"You are so fucking mean." Mika shakes her head.

"Okay, everyone get into your positions. We are going to go over how to throw a punch without breaking your thumb!" Jake says from the front of the room.

Thirty minutes later, I'm sweating in places I never dreamed I'd sweat in while in Alaska.

His workouts are intense to say the least but I think I finally have a hang on how to throw multiple punches non-stop, even when my arms feel like spaghetti.

"How'd you like your first class?" Jake walks up with the other girls as I'm wiping the sweat from my head.

"It was fun but I bet I'll be hurting in the morning?" I laugh.

"You'll be used to it in no time. You'll be so badass no one will mess with you, not even Glitch." Arin smiles.

"Glitch? You've met Glitch?" Mika raises a brow.

"Sort of." I shrug.

"He yelled at her at the park today. Demanding to know who she was and why she had the kids." Arin frowns.

"What? I will totally beat his ass!" Mika says, getting worked up on my behalf.

"No worries. I gave him a talking to so he won't soon forget." Arin grins.

"I don't want him hating me." I say nervously, wanting to be friends with everyone they are friends with too.

"Oh, trust me. You're a woman. That man doesn't hate you." Jake laughs but stops quickly when Cass elbows him in the ribs.

Thinking that I probably know his meaning but not wanting to comment on it, I stuff my towel into my bag.

"You all ready to go eat? I worked off enough calories and I need to replenish." Arin slaps her hands together, walking towards the door.

"You know that is not the purpose of a workout right?" Jake asks as he and Cass follow her.

"Come on. I'm starving." Mika smiles, taking my arm, leading us in the same direction.

Chapter 3

Glitch

I waited all through Church last night for the Prez to mention Arin's new babysitter but he never did.

So after Church, I tried to ask him about her but all he said was that we were to keep an eye on her. Make sure she was getting on okay being in a new place.

He wouldn't give me any other information on her at all. Not even where she is from.

Knowing that I wasn't satisfied with anything he did say, he made me swear on the club that I wouldn't try to find out anything about her.

Of course all that did was make more questions pop up in my mind. There has to be a damn good reason that the Prez would make me swear such a thing.

I know Taylor works a lot of domestic type cases like divorces and even adoptions but surely something of that nature wouldn't be top secret like we are in the pentagon.

For now, I'll keep my word and not look her up. However, I did not swear that I wouldn't talk to the woman herself. Most people let small tiny pieces of information slip out without even realizing it.

Besides, I can't say I wouldn't mind seeing her again. Her feisty behavior stayed in my mind so much that it gave me a hard on while I was taking a shower last night.

Jerking off to a woman I don't even know isn't something I normally do.

I like feeling the real thing wrapped around my cock. But last night, imagining her being sassy with me as I pounded in and out of her had me blowing a load so big I thought my windows in my cabin would blow out.

Parking my bike on the side street, I make my way to the stairs leading up to the apartment above the Poison Pen shop.

Hopefully, the girls of Poison Pen didn't hear me coming. I don't want them to interrupt me while I'm telling a beautiful woman I'm sorry for how I reacted to her having the kids at the park.

Taking the stairs two at a time, I stand in front of the door longer than normal as if I'm nervous.

"Man up, fuck!" I whisper to myself as I knock on the door.

A few seconds later the door swings open revealing the woman that's been on my mind the last few days.

"Glitch. What are you doing here?" She asks, looking behind her nervously.

"I wanted to come by and say that I'm sorry for jumping on your case the other day. I just didn't know who you were and you had the kids. Kids I consider family." I shrug.

"Well, um, I appreciate that. Thank you." She says, looking back at me for several long seconds. "Would you like to come in? The kids are taking a nap so you'll have to be quiet."

"Sure. I can be as quiet or as loud as you want me to be." I whisper back at her with a grin.

She looks taken aback for a second before she opens the door wider and I walk inside. It looks basically the same as it did when Arin lived here before her and Taylor moved in together.

I follow Shelby into the kitchen area and take a seat at the table.

"Would you like a drink?" She asks, fidgeting with her hands.

That's when I notice how shaky she is and wonder if she has issues with her sugar getting low.

"Hey, you okay?" I ask, standing up to look at her as she opens a cabinet where I assume the glasses are at.

"Yeah. I'm fine." She comments, reaching up above her head.

"Here, let me." I say, walking quickly over to help but she jumps as I move so I slow my movements. Reaching up, I grab two glasses and hand them to her. "These work?"

"Yes. Thank you." She looks down, not looking me in the eyes.

Her reaction worries me. Where's the woman from the other day? The one that was willing to go toe to toe with me at the park.

Walking back to the table, I take a seat, hoping that it'll help to calm her but her reaction truly bothers me. It's as if she's scared of me and I don't fucking like it.

She comes over to the table, sitting our glasses down in front of us and I notice it's red.

"Kool-Aid." She shrugs with a small giggle. "That's all I have."

"It's more than fine." I smile, picking it and drinking it. "God, that takes me back to when I was a kid."

"Right? My nanny used to make it for me when my parents were gone somewhere. It's the only time I could have it as my mom didn't like me having a lot of sugar." She laughs, shaking her head.

"Was your mom strict?" I ask.

"Not really. She was just super conscientious about sugar rotting the teeth. She was a great mom though. When she was there." She smiles. "What about your parents? Were they strict?"

"Not really. My dad was in the Army. He was gone a lot but even when he came back it was great."

"An Army brat, huh?" She smiles.

Her fidgeting with her hands still hasn't stopped and I noticed that she rarely looks me straight in the eyes although she's trying her best to act normal.

"Yep. Army brat. Mom passed away a few years ago but dad still lives up around Fort Wainwright. I visit as often as I can. Do you stay in touch with your parents?"

My question causes her lip to quiver slightly.

"They passed away quite a few years ago." She quietly says.

Reaching my hand over, I lay it on her own and she quickly pulls away. I start to apologize when we hear little feet moving around in the other room.

"The kids are waking up." She moves from the table.

"Guess I'll go. I have some stuff that I'm supposed to be taking care of anyway. Prez is probably blowing my phone up." I get up from the table too.

"Prez?" She asks.

"Yeah, that's what we call the man in charge of our club. His name is Eagle. I'm sure you'll meet him eventually. He's Atka's brother."

"Oh. Yeah, I'm sure I will. Mika was talking about having a cookout soon and inviting everyone."

Getting to the door, I open it and step outside, turning back to look at her.

"I'll see you later, I'm sure." I grin one last time as I walk away.

Getting to the bottom of the stairs, I look back up at her as she is still watching me so I give her my best grin as I pull my shades over my eyes. Turning away, I head back to my bike.

I may not have learned a lot but I did learn a few things from talking to her. For some reason that woman is scared.

She's scared and it pisses me the fuck off. I want to see the feisty woman from the other day all the time, not just in public.

Shelby

Once the door shuts behind Glitch, I try to slow my breathing before heading into the room with the kids. I tried my best to hide the shaking, to act normal but it was so hard.

He seems like a really great guy and I wouldn't say that I'm afraid of him exactly. I wasn't even really afraid of him at the park. It's just here, in my own space, alone with him, I was nervous of what he could do to me.

It would probably help immensely if I went to therapy for how I've felt since finally getting away from Grey. I don't think that every man in the world is like him, I know they aren't but they have the potential to be which is what I'm afraid of.

What if I try again with someone new and they wind up acting exactly like Grey. He hid it long enough that by the time it all started happening, I was in too deep to leave and I hate to admit it but I somehow held on to the faith that it would stop.

It didn't stop though. It got worse. He was trying his best to kill me in that courtroom and would have succeeded if there hadn't been other people there to stop the assault.

Taylor told me that they should place a huge bond on him before he's allowed out but I know my ex-husband, he has plenty of money and he will get out. When he does, he's very likely to come after me or the children.

That's why I didn't put up much of a fight about coming to Alaska. No one knows I'm here and hopefully no one finds out. Especially Grey.

A shiver runs through my body at the thought of him coming here, catching me unaware. I'll be prepared this time though. I pay close attention during self defense class and even workout on my own late at night after my sweet babies have gone to sleep.

"Mom?" I hear Bryson call from the other room.

"I'm coming sweetheart." Gathering myself, I put a smile on my face and go to the kids.

Glitch

After leaving Shelby's apartment, I head towards Taylor's office hoping that he's there. Pulling up out front, I park my Bike on the sidewalk, hanging my helmet on the handlebars.

As I walk in, Maria West, Taylor's secretary looks up from her computer and grins sheepishly at me.

She's the reason I usually try to avoid coming here. She makes it completely obvious she's interested but she's never turned my head at all. It's not that she isn't beautiful, she is, she's just the type that would expect way more than I would be willing to give to her.

She would never be the one woman to wear the patch claiming her as mine to the entire world. All I would ever be able to offer her is a good fuck, maybe two before I'd be ready to move on somewhere else.

Shelby's face flashes in mind and it stops me for only a second.

"Hi, Glitch. What are you doing here?" Maria asks sweetly, twirling a strand of her hair in her fingers and poking her breasts out even more than normal. I do my best not to roll my eyes.

"Is Taylor in?" I ask, not smiling back as I don't want to encourage her at all although it doesn't seem to affect her.

"Yes, let me see if he's busy." She picks up her phone and I turn away to look at the picture on the wall.

A few minutes later, I hear Taylor's office door open.

"Glitch! Come on back man. Have a seat." He says as I walk into the room. "What can I do for you today?"

"Shelby."

"What about her?" His face goes serious and he leans back in his chair.

"What's her story?" I ask, getting to the point.

Leaning forward, he looks me straight in my eyes. "Care to tell me what this is all about?" He avoids my question.

"Look, man, I'm just wondering about her. She..." I hold my hands out. "Intrigues me."

"She intrigues you?" He laughs, shaking his head. "She's not for you, man. Trust me."

"Hey, she might be the love of my life." I say and he laughs even harder.

"Lord help whatever woman does fall in love with you."

"Now that's just fucking mean." I laugh. "Seriously though, I was around her the other day at the park and she wasn't the least bit afraid to put me in my place."

He raises his brows, "Really?" He seems surprised.

"Yeah but then I went to her apartment..."

"What? Why the fuck would you go to her apartment?" He demands, narrowing his eyes at me.

"I went to apologize for the way I acted at the park."

"And just how did you act at the park? Did you scare her?" He stands up quickly.

"Jesus man, would you let me just telling the fucking story? I didn't scare her. At least it didn't seem like I did. She was feisty and fierce. I went to the apartment earlier to apologize but this time she seemed more shaky. This time it was like she was afraid of me and I want to know why."

He looks at me for so long that I'm afraid he's not going to say anything at all.

"Shelby's had a hard life." He says.

I wait for him to continue but he doesn't.

"Seriously? That's all you're gonna say?"

"If Shelby wants to tell you then so be it but it's her story to tell. Not mine. Just don't go back to the apartment again. I mean it. Don't make me get your Prez to push the matter."

"Really you asshole? Threaten me with Eagle?" I demand as he laughs.

"It works though, doesn't it?" He asks but starts laughing when I flip him off as I head out of his office.

I'm almost to the door when Maria stops me.

"Glitch?" She asks and I turn back to look at her with a raised brow. "I wanted to ask if you'd like to have a drink with me sometime?"

Barely holding back from telling her what I really think, I give her a polite smile. "Sorry but I'm a little busy these days."

"Oh well, maybe some other time?"

"Maybe." I say, turning to the door and leaving.

That maybe will definitely never fucking happen though. That's the kind of woman that comes with trouble and I'm not interested.

Getting on my bike, I head back to the clubhouse.

Chapter 4

Shelby

The last few days have been hectic, with preparations for the Poison Pen picnic. Arin is running around like a chicken with her head cut off. Cass keeps reassuring her that everything is perfect and Mika is laughing at both of them.

I can understand Arin's anxiety, not only is her daughter coming for her yearly visit, her mentor and Boss Fiona is coming. I am intimidated by Fiona and I've never met the woman but from everything the girls tell me about her, she is scary.

Keeping the kids out of the way while the final touches are added is my job until people start showing up. Thank goodness this area is fenced in otherwise I would lose my mind trying to keep up with them.

When Olivia shrieks, "Sissy" and runs into the arms of a teenage girl I start to go after her but Mika puts her hand on my shoulder and stops me.

"You are officially off the clock. That's Arin's daughter." She tells me.

I have to do a double take. I know Arin was only fifteen when she was forced to give up her daughter for adoption but this girl seems too old to belong to Arin.

Naomi puts Olivia back on her feet and Olivia grabs her hand pulling her towards the sandbox where the younger kids are playing.

"Sissy. Come ons. You gotsa meet my boyfwiend." I hear her saying. "This is Bwyson, he is gonna marry me when I gets older."

Bryson gives the girls a scowl, "I am not! Girls have cooties."

"Yes you are!" Olivia stomps her foot and crosses her arms. "My mommy says boys gotta listen to girls and I'm a girl so you gotsa do what I say!"

Instead of responding further my smart little man asks her, "You wanna build a sand castle?"

"But you said I gots cooties." Olivia pouts.

"Cooties don't like sand," Bryson replies.

All of the adults that witness their interaction are laughing their asses off as Olivia drags her big sister into the sandbox to build sandcastles.

I'm still watching the kids when movement out of the corner of my eye makes me jump. Relaxing when I realize it is just Mika trying to get my attention I feel embarrassed. Everything has been going so well but being around all these strangers is making me jumpy.

"Come sit with me," Mika says.

"I can't, the kids might need me," I answer.

"Naomi is on kid duty now, besides look around you. See that tall bald guy with the leather jacket and tattoo of an eagle on his neck." She points to a big scary guy that is standing by the entrance.

"That is my brother-in-law Eagle. All these guys wearing leather jackets even though it's hot as hell out here today, they answer to him. There is no way anyone is going to get in or out of here without him knowing. This is the safest place to be in Alaska today."

I don't agree that it's "hot as hell out here" but being pregnant probably makes it seem hotter than it actually is. If we were back home in California then it probably would be hot, but the temperatures here are comfortable. I am kind of worried about what the winter months are going to be like.

I'm reluctant to let the kids out of my sight but Mika's words do ease some of the tension thrumming through my body. Following her to a shady spot that Atka set up for her, I keep glancing over my shoulder to check on the kids.

Picking a chair that gives me a direct line of sight to where the kids are playing, we both get comfortable and I listen as Mika points out different people and explains to me who they are.

We laugh as she tells me stories about the MC guys, especially the one they call Mac. Apparently, he's a six-foot-five-inch tall Scottish bartender that always wears a kilt.

It was windy outside the first time Mika saw Mac get on his motorcycle. That's how she discovered he doesn't wear anything under his kilt.

I'm laughing so hard the chair underneath me nearly tips over, when she leans closer and tells me, "It is a view you need to see to believe."

"Mika!" I scold jokingly. "You are a married woman."

"Married not dead." She replies trying to keep a straight face but failing.

We're lost in our conversation when the sound of a throat clearing startles me.

"Excuse me ladies," Atka addresses both of us. "Goddess, are you hungry?"

I've heard the story of their first meeting, so I giggle when he calls Mika, Goddess. He walked in on her while she was showering and fell to his knees. I don't blame the guy one bit at this late stage of her pregnancy, Mika looks like a Fertility Goddess.

I tune them out and look over at the sandbox to check on the kids, but they aren't there. Gasping for breath, I'm ready to jump out of my seat but Mika grabs my arm.

"Calm down Mama Bear, they are right there." She points to a table that has been set up just for the kids.

Lowering my face into my hands, I shove my palm into my mouth to muffle a scream of rage. Greyson Porter has taken so much from me that I panic just from losing sight of my kids for one damn minute.

"Hey, hey hey, it's okay." Mika tries to assure me.

"No, it's not!" I snap. Instantly I know my words shouldn't have come out like that. Mika doesn't deserve my anger.

"I'm sorry, Mika." I apologize before standing up. "I'm really sorry. I just need a minute. Can you ..." I can't even finish asking as tears stream down my face.

Atka cautiously approaches me, "Go Shelby, I got my eyes on the kids. Take a few minutes for yourself."

"Thank you," I tell them both before pushing my way through the picnickers. Knowing strangers are watching me fall apart, makes me move faster.

I walk into the shop and go straight to the storage room in the back. I could have gone upstairs but with so many unknown people around, I don't want them to see me go into the apartment.

The storage room is the only place I can think of where there shouldn't be any people. It's dark and quiet as I lean my back against the wall and slide down to sit on the floor. For the first time since arriving in Alaska, I absolutely lose control.

I'm sobbing so hard that I don't even hear the door open and close, not realizing someone has joined me until I feel an arm wrap around my shoulders.

I jump and try to scramble away but the arm only holds on tighter. It takes a moment for me to recognize Arin's voice.

Relaxing into her, Arin does her best to comfort me, she just holds me and allows me to cry on her shoulder.

Once my tears slow down, Arin breaks her silence. "I want you to meet someone." She says it at the same moment I realize we aren't alone.

I look up to see a woman that reminds me of the character Lara Croft from that Tomb Raider movie, except this woman has tattoos covering her from the neck down.

She is leaning against the door with her arms crossed as if she is preventing anyone from entering.

"This is my boss." She starts but the woman interrupts, "Sister."

Arin gives her a look but continues, "This is my sister Fiona."

Apparently, that was Fiona's cue to step in, "Who upset you?" She demands. "You tell me who's ass I need to kick!"

"No..nobody's ass needs kicking. I just freaked out. The kids were playing then I looked away for just a minute but when I looked back they were gone. I almost lost it but they only moved over to the table for food." I explain.

"Why does not seeing the kids scare you?" She asks next.

I look at Arin first, and when she nods her head I answer, "My ex-husband Greyson, he hurt my son. When the judge gave me full custody he attacked me and he..." I pause to take a breath. "He said some things to me. When he had his hands around my throat, trying to kill me, he said he was going to take them and never let me see them again."

At this, Arin gasped. "Shelby! Did you tell Taylor this?"

"No," I lower my head. "I mean, I assumed Taylor heard him but everything was crazy. The bailiff and Taylor were trying to pull him off of me, the Judge was shouting over everyone and I just needed to get out of there."

When Arin says, "Well that explains a few things." I look between her and Fiona in confusion.

"What?" I ask as Arin starts laughing.

She looks at Fiona, "You know how the MC guys pretty much adopted all the Poison Pen kids as honorary nieces and nephews?"

"Yeah?" Fiona questions.

"Well, they call Shelby, Mama Bear and half of them are too scared to get near the kids when she's watching them."

"Wait a minute!" I exclaim. "Outside, just before I came in here, Mika called me Mama Bear."

Fiona slaps her hand against her thigh and laughs, "This I gotta see! Girl, Arin has been telling me about our new sister for months now. If you have those guys scared of you, you are definitely one of us. Now come on, let's go eat."

She holds her hand out to help me up and pulls me in for a hug before the three of us walk out of the storage room. "Go to the bathroom and splash some cold water on your face. You got this." She says right before the scariest man I have ever seen pulls her away from me.

I watch in awe as she wraps her arms around his neck and moves up on the tips of her toes to kiss him. "Baratta baby, meet my new sister. This is Shelby."

With one arm he pulls her close and with the other, he extends his hand as if to shake. When I flinch away, he pulls it back.

"Who is he?" Baratta demands.

I'm confused, "Who is who?"

"Who scared you so much, you won't even shake my hand?"

Fiona whispers something in his ear but he's too focused on me.

"If this man is a danger to my family, you better tell me who he is right now!" I would pull back but Arin stops me and steps up in his face.

"Baratta, I love you but if you don't chill and stop scaring her right now, I will kick your ass all the way back to Montana!" Arin orders him.

It's not even that he backs down that snaps me out of my fear. The fact that this giant of a man just backed down from tiny little Arin, is what hits me. Neither of these women is afraid of him.

I surprise myself when I answer his original question. "Greyson Porter is my ex-husband. He's not a threat to anyone but me. The last time I saw him he was being hauled away in handcuffs but I don't know if he's still locked up or not."

"I can take care of him for you," Baratta tells me.

Wait what? Did he just offer to kill my ex? "Um no, thank you. He is the father of my kids, even though he treated me like shit the kids deserve a chance to know him."

"Baratta! You can't just say things like that." Fiona says.

"Why not? You said she's family now. We protect our family." He asks.

Fiona puts her hands on her hips, "That man is the father of her children."

"You're right," He almost sounds sad that I'm not asking him to kill Grey. "If you ever change your mind, you call me."

We talk for a few minutes but Fiona's attention is in high demand and she is pulled away. So, I make my way back out to check on the kids. It's been too long since I saw them with my own eyes. I know they are safely surrounded by the Poison Pen family but I still need that reassurance.

The things Arin told me, keep running through my head. When I step outside and look around, I spot a few of the MC guys pushing the kids on the swings but as I get closer to the kids, the guys are moving further away or wandering off.

Could it be true that they are scared of me? Only one of the guys didn't run away. He is standing at the end of the swing set banging on a cross beam with a set of drumsticks.

"Hey, Mama Bear." He calls out. "I'm Sticks. Naomi had to go help her Mom."

I'm confused for a second because I just left Arin, but then it hits me that he means her adoptive mom. We talk for a few minutes but he's soon called away by Eagle to help with cleaning up.

People are starting to leave and I notice Bryson and Dyna look worn out. Scooping them into my arms, we say our goodbyes before heading to the apartment.

Chapter 5

Glitch

Watching from a distance is getting old. I've kept an eye on Shelby since we met, so I see when she flinches away from people, mostly men. It pisses me off and I barely know this woman. Something keeps pulling me to her.

Riding my bike down the street, suddenly she is there taking the kids for a walk. Grocery shopping, she is there. If I didn't know she was scared shitless of men, I would think she was stalking me.

I decided a long time ago that I didn't want kids, so why am I attracted to a woman with two little crotch goblins? Even more confusing is, why am I wondering how she would look filled with my baby?

Watching over her during the picnic, I saw every time she jumped or flinched away from people.

When she panicked and ran inside, I tried to follow her but it seemed like everyone needed something from me along the way.

When I finally get inside the building and track her down she is talking to Arin, Fiona, and Baratta.

This is the first time I've seen her have a conversation with a man that wasn't me, so I hold back. Yes, I admit, I'm nosey.

I can't hear most of what she is saying but the name Greyson Porter is loud and clear.

I need more information. Taylor can't tell me anything because he is her lawyer. Eagle knows more than he's saying and Arin would rip me a new asshole if I tried getting information out of her.

Since Shelby is in good hands, I slip back outside instead of approaching her. Pulling out my cell phone, I type Greyson Porter in the search engine. The information that comes up has me gripping my phone so hard, I can hear it crack.

Mostly it brings up gossip sites, but one that sticks out is a court report. I read about how Greyson Porter jumped the table and attacked his ex-wife Shelby Nicholson in the courtroom when he wasn't granted custody of their minor children.

Deciding that the only way to get the full picture is to go to the source, I find Eagle and let him know I'm going to be gone for a week on personal business. He's curious but I don't give him any answers so he walks off to organize the guys on clean-up duty.

I can't go anywhere without checking on Shelby one more time. I find her watching the kids play and Sticks is talking to her.

I wonder if he notices that she is edging away from him as he talks. She seems relieved when Eagle calls Sticks away and puts him to work. Once she starts up the stairs with the kids, I head for the airport.

Normally getting a last-minute flight out of Anchorage would be a hassle but having my pilot's license and my own small plane means I only have to file a flight plan. I'm not rich by any means but I made some good investments.

My little four-seater gets me where I need to go. Maybe I'll take Shelby up to see the northern lights when I get back. Distracted by that thought, I have to remind myself to focus on the paperwork in front of me.

It doesn't take long and soon I'm on the tarmac doing a safety check, fueling up and waiting for a runway.

It will take me around six hours to fly to Seattle where I'll refuel and get some sleep before I head out again for Los Angeles.

The second stretch will take me approximately seven hours, so I need to book a room in both Seattle and LA. That doesn't even take up to five minutes and I'm still waiting for clearance to take off.

Killing time by doing more research on Porter is only making me more eager to get in the air. I need to focus on the plane so I have to shut off my phone. Otherwise, I might miss something important.

The first leg of the flight runs smoothly. I'm exhausted but along the way realized I better call ahead. I wouldn't want any of the LA motorcycle clubs to think I'm there to cause trouble for them.

I didn't want Eagle to know what I'm up to but I need to call him to see if he has any contacts there. If I lie to him he can take my patch, but I know he won't like me digging either. Sometimes it's better to ask forgiveness than permission.

Somehow I get the information I need without giving away too much but I can tell that I'm going to have to tell him everything when I get back. My next call goes much easier.

Ward, the President of the Vagabonds MC even offers to have someone meet me at the airport so I don't have to rent a cage. Finally able to relax, I sleep for four hours before getting back up in the air. There is a little turbulence before landing in LA but nothing I can't handle.

Once I deplane, I'm met by three guys wearing Vagabond cuts. A cut is a leather vest with a club patch on it.

Ward steps forward and introduces himself.

"You must be Glitch. I'm Ward the Vagabonds Prez." Then he introduces the two men with him. "This is Stretch," He points to the tall guy on his left. "And this is Keys. I had an interesting call from Eagle this morning. He said you were being cagey about your reasons for being here. If you can't be honest with me, you can get right back on that plane and get out of my town."

Deciding to be honest with him even if it gets back to Eagle, I tell him, "I'm here to find out everything I can about Greyson Porter."

Stretch lets out a growl, interrupting me. "What do you need to know about that piece of shit?"

"I need to know if he's a threat to the woman I intend to make mine!" I snap.

Stretch tosses a keychain to Keys, "Take my bike." He tells him before turning to me, "Get in the cage with me I'll tell you everything I know on the way to the clubhouse."

Leading me to a jacked-up truck, we watch Ward and Keys take off on bikes. I hate cages but Stretch has something to tell me and we can't do that on bikes.

As soon as my seatbelt clicks, he hits the gas and tears out of the parking lot, barely slowing to go through the gate.

Whatever he has to say must piss him off, so I decide to wait for him to start the conversation.

He takes the ramp onto the highway before he opens up. "Greyson Porter is a scumbag." he starts.

"He started out as a talent scout about fifteen years ago. Traveled around to colleges watching performances, visited local bars to hear live bands and stuff like that. The man knows how to schmooze people.

Seven years ago, the first time he heard my little sister sing, he started pursuing her. Claimed he was going to make her a star. It only took him a few days to talk his way into her panties. Ellie was doing good, she didn't hit it big or anything but she was following her dreams and happy. Or so I thought.

We used to talk every week then suddenly, she was only calling me once a month. I bought a ticket to her show and surprised her backstage. Ellie didn't have her makeup done yet and when I walked into the dressing room she kept pulling her hair down over her eyes, hiding her face from me." Stretch's knuckles are white as he grips the steering wheel. I don't dare interrupt him.

"I pushed her hands away to find a black eye. She refused to tell me who did it. That bastard charged into the dressing room to see why she wasn't ready yet and lifted his hand to her, but stopped himself when he realized I was there. I wanted to take him out right then and there but she begged me not to. About a week later she called me crying because he left her for some hotshot actor's kid.

I let it go, he was out of Ellie's life and she was able to move on. She's happy and has a family now, but then I heard through the grapevine about the shit he pulled on his wife and I regret not following through. No woman deserves to be treated that way." He takes a deep breath, "I blame myself for letting him live. If you need anything, let me know."

"This," I tell him. "This is what I need, access to a computer would be great but I also need to talk to people that know him or knew him. If she never pressed charges, I won't find out this kind of information no matter how deep I dig online."

Arriving at the Vagabond's clubhouse he leads me to a computer room. "This is Keys' domain as long as you don't touch his personal computer he won't mind giving you access. We have a room here where you can crash and I'll make phone calls to see if I can introduce you to some people."

"You sure this is okay with your Prez? I don't wanna step on any toes." I ask him.

"Is what okay with me?" Ward asks, walking up behind me.

While Stretch fills him in, I look over the computer equipment. It seems to be exactly like my setup back home. Once I have Ward's approval I crack my knuckles and get to work.

Everything I find online, I could have found from my own system back home but Like I told Stretch, the personal stories, the times charges weren't pressed, I can't find those on a computer screen.

For the next three days, I dig through cyberspace with the occasional break to meet up with someone that has agreed to talk to me. By the time I'm ready to return home, I know everything there is to know about Greyson Porter.

Between money he borrowed against Shelby's trust fund and the trail of abused women he left behind, Greyson Porter has to die. I would happily take him out while I'm in LA but nobody seems to know where he is.

The only conclusion I can come to is that he is using cash. If he was using credit cards, I'd be able to trace his location. After making bail, he took out a big loan and disappeared.

Hitting dead ends isn't productive, so after setting up alerts on his cards and cell phone I pack up and ask Stretch for a ride back to the airport.

He hangs around while I file my flight plan and do my maintenance checks before he leaves.

"Thanks for your help, man." I tell him, shaking his hand. "If you ever need anything, call me, I owe you one."

"You don't owe me anything, just take out the trash if the opportunity comes up." He answers me.

As I'm taxiing down the runway, I notice Stretch is still watching, so I give him a salute before taking off. I want to fly straight home, but my little plane isn't built to be in the air that long. So I find myself once again in Seattle.

Only landing long enough to refuel, check the weather, and grab something to eat, I'm back up in the air less than two hours after landing. I know I shouldn't fly like this and if Eagle finds out I'm going to be punished but not knowing where Greyson Porter is, makes my skin itch.

The whole time I was in LA I probably only slept about four hours a night. By the time I'm back on the ground in Anchorage, I'm ready to become reacquainted with my pillow.

Stumbling into the Midnight Son's clubhouse at two in the morning I drop the folder of all my findings on Eagle's desk and go directly to my bunk. I'm going to ask Shelby on a date, is the last thought that runs through my head before I close my eyes.

By the time I wake up the day is almost gone but I refuse to wait one more minute. Quickly showering and getting dressed, I'm running out the door when I hear Eagle call my name.

"Dammit! I almost made it out." I mumble as I turn around.

Eagle lifts his eyebrows at me but pretends he didn't hear what I said. "You got a minute?" He asks, not waiting for an answer before going to his office. Since I don't have a death wish, I follow him.

I close the door as he sits behind his desk and opens the folder I left for him. "I found some interesting information on my desk this morning. You wanna tell me how it got here?"

"Prez." I begin. "In that folder is everything I found on Shelby's ex-husband. The flash drive contains recordings of my interviews with his victims. I believe Greyson Porter is a threat to Shelby's life and since she works for Poison Pen it is our responsibility to look out for her."

"Oh and you did all this research just because she works for my sister?" He questions.

"No sir," I know better than to lie to Eagle. "I am going to make her mine and I need to know what has spooked her. You either couldn't or wouldn't share any info."

Now he looks like he's a combination of amused and pissed off. Maybe I shouldn't have said that last sentence out loud.

"Let's get a couple of things straight. First I only knew that she had been abused and attacked, I was not made aware of the seriousness of the threat. Until you left this on my desk I don't think anyone was aware of the full situation. Second, you did this knowing the club needed your plane to do a drop in Ketchikan two days ago. You informed me that you needed some personal time but at no point did you tell anyone you were flying out of state."

"Oh shit, I forgot. I'm sorry Prez. I'll fix it."

"It's covered, we hired a pilot but his pay is coming out of your share. You know I have to punish you, right?" He asks me.

"Yes sir, I'll take whatever punishment you give me." I answer.

I watch as Eagle considers his words, "You will scrub the Eagle's Nest toilets with a toothbrush, every day for a week. When you're not scrubbing toilets you are to be Shelby's personal bodyguard anytime she leaves the apartment."

"Yes, Prez." There is nothing else to say.

"Now get out of here. You start tomorrow morning." He tells me, making a shooing motion.

I'm halfway out the door when he calls out, "Oh and Glitch, you know she's a package deal right? Seems I recall you talking about getting the goods clipped so you couldn't have kids."

"The little crotch goblins kind of grow on you." I shrug. "Talked to Doc about the surgery, but couldn't go through with it."

Eagle starts laughing, "You, who I have seen face down an armed man, is scared of having a little surgery?"

"You can see a bullet coming for you, Prez. Who the hell knows what a Docs gonna do to your body while you're knocked out."

I can still hear him laughing as the door closes behind me. Rubbing my hands together, I head out and jump on my bike to hunt down my prey.

My first stop is the apartment, nobody is there. Next, I poke my head in at Poison Pen. Cass is behind the reception desk. Mika is sitting in a chair with her feet up and Arin is working on a customer.

"Hey ladies," I address all of them. "Anyone know where I can find Shelby?"

"Why?" Cass is the first to ask.

"I'm going to ask her on a date." I don't hesitate to answer. I know how these women watch out for each other.

"It's about fucking time!" Arin calls from her workstation. "You've been eyeballing her for weeks now."

"If you waited much longer, I was going to ask Atka and some of the guys to help you find your balls," Mika says, giving me a dirty look.

"And when will this date take place?" Cass asks me.

"Well, I mean, soon." I'm lost for words. These women are scary as hell so when they tell me to sit, I sit.

"Shelby should be back in a few minutes, so we gotta talk fast," Arin says as she leaves her customer at the front desk with Cass.

"You on your bike?" She asks me.

"Of course," I answer not knowing where this is going.

"When she gets here, you'll ask her to go on a date tonight. If you give her time to think about it, she's going to say no. We aren't going to give her the chance." Arin explains.

"The Outlook steak house on Seward Highway is casual." Mika rubs her hands together.

"I met the owner," Cass adds to the conversation. "I'll call ahead for you and get a table on the balcony."

"I'll take the kids for the night." Arin is saying as Shelby opens the front door.

She looks at each of us as she pushes the stroller inside. "And why are you taking the kids?" She asks Arin.

"I'm taking your kids for the night because you are going on a date with Glitch and then if all my prayers are answered he's going to rock your world." Arin answers.

I watch as Shelby tilts her head, "Why would that answer your prayers?"

"Because then I'll have blackmail material." Arins says with a cartoon style evil laugh, "Mwah hahaha."

I follow as Arin pulls Shelby out to my bike.

"But, I need to shower and change. Arin, I'm not dressed to go on a date." Shelby insists.

But Arin only says, "Too bad, so sad." as she puts my helmet on Shelby and walks away.

"Umm, I don't think they are going to let either one of us back inside." I say as I watch Arin lock the door behind her.

"I've never been on a motorcycle before," Shelby tells me.

"I'll be careful just sit behind me and wrap your arms around my waist." I instruct her as I get on my bike and wait for her to join me.

Once she gives in, I adjust her arms and we take off. She is stiff at first but I can tell the moment she relaxes and starts to enjoy the ride.

The Outlook restaurant is twenty miles out of town on a cliff that overlooks a waterfall in the National forest. You would think it would be a place for the snobby rich tourist but they prefer to cater to locals so the dress code is casual.

As soon as I park, I'm off the bike offering Shelby a hand. With it being her first time I expect her legs to be wobbly and I'm right. Her knees buckle as soon as she tries to stand up.

I grab her hips to hold her steady until she can feet under her. "I'm good," She says after a minute.

Neither of us has much to say until we are seated on the balcony. "Once the server walks away Shelby looks at me and says, "I feel like we got ambushed."

"Yeah I wanted to ask you out but I don't have your number. If you don't want to be here, I completely understand. I can take you home." I nervously start to stand up.

"No," She puts her hand on my arm. "We're already here and the view is breathtaking."

Settling back down, I can't take my eyes off of her. "Yes, it is."

Through dinner, we talk and get to know each other better. She's not surprised when I tell her I grew up out in the wilderness. It wasn't until I was eighteen that I moved to town.

"You kind of have that lumberjack vibe." She tells me, laughing.

She is surprised though when I tell her I'm a pilot and a hacker.

"Really? How do those things go together?" She asks.

"There is an abundance of two things in Alaska. Open skies and open roads. My dad was a pilot in the military and after returning from war in one of those countries that is always fighting somebody, he moved here. With nothing but a rucksack and a pilot's license. Met my mom and made me. Mom decided having a kid was a prison, so she took off leaving me behind with a man that never could keep his feet on the ground. I learned to fly before I could spell my own name.

"And the other stuff?" She encourages me to continue when I pause.

"Adhd," I laugh. "If I wasn't in the Pilot's seat, I couldn't sit still. I had to keep my hands moving and my brain engaged otherwise I got into trouble. Computers and hacking just clicked. It wasn't enough but then I got my first motorcycle. I was flying without leaving the ground."

Dinner seemed to last for hours but was over in the blink of an eye. I didn't want the night to end so invited her to join me for a drink at Eagle's Nest. Instead of being nervous, she is eager to ride my bike again.

Flying down the highway with Shelby's arms around me feels right. I jump when she wiggles around and accidentally runs her hand over my cock, but when it happens a second and then a third time I start thinking it's not an accident.

I'm glad the drive is almost over or I'm going to cream my pants like a teenage boy, but I also wish we had farther to go because I never want her hands off me.

Not wanting the guys to see me, I park in the alley beside Poison Pen instead of the bar. If we walk from here, maybe my cock won't be so obvious. The shop is closed up and nobody is around this time of night.

Taking her helmet off Shelby asks me, "I thought we were going to the bar?"

"So did I but once you put your hands on my cock, that idea went by the roadside," I answer her.

"Oh sorry," She says with her face turning red. Looking down at the ground she continues, "The vibrations from the bike and your body, so close to mine."

She bites her bottom lip. "It's been a while and ..."

"Shelby!" I say firmly to get her attention. "You can touch any part of me, anytime you want."

"Really?" she questions. "So if I wanted to kiss you, it would be okay?"

"It would be more than okay." I lean closer and take her lips in mine.

When she relaxes into the kiss, I grab her by her hips, lifting her off the ground and setting her on the seat of my bike. She clings to me, wrapping her arms around my neck and her legs around my waist as if she's afraid I'll back away.

Sliding my hands up under her shirt, the feel of her soft skin makes my cock harder than it's ever been. My hands continue their journey up and under her bra until I find myself cupping her tits and gently squeezing them.

Not releasing my prize, I flick her nipples with my thumbs until they are rock hard. She moans into my mouth demanding more. Pulling away from her lips is difficult but I must taste her breasts.

I clumsily push her shirt and bra up, exposing her chest to me. She pulls her shoulders back and thrust her tits forward, it's an invitation I can't refuse.

Licking and sucking first one nipple, then the other I can't help thinking how perfect they are. Releasing her tits from my grip. I slide my hands around to her back and down to the waistband of her pants.

Pushing both hands under her panties, I grab one perfect ass cheek in each hand.

I'm still licking and sucking at her tits as I pull her close, grinding my cock against her opening through our clothes.

Stunned is the only way to describe how I feel when first she screams her release and moments later I blow my load in my pants.

I pull my hands out of her pants but don't release her as she sags into me. Lifting her off the bike, I carry her upstairs. "Where's your keys, darling?" I ask at the door to her apartment.

She whispers something, but it's too low for me to hear. "Huh?" I ask.

"In my pocket," She finally answers.

With her arms still locked around my neck, I reach into her pocket for the key and let us in. I remember the floor plan of the apartment so take her straight to the bedroom on the left and hope I chose the correct room. I did.

Setting her down on the edge of her bed, I drop down on my knees between her legs. She hasn't made eye contact with me since getting off and I need to make sure she's okay with everything that happened.

"Shelby, look at me," I tell her, then wait patiently for her to lift her head.

Once she makes eye contact, I ask, "What's wrong sweetheart?"

"I...I've never done anything like that before. I was only ever with Greyson. Sex with him was like ..." She thinks for a minute before continuing. "It wasn't anything like that. It wasn't fun or exciting or... Oh My God Glitch! Arin has cameras on the outside of the building!"

"Well, then I guess she won't have to ask for anything to blackmail me with." I laugh.

"You don't mind that she might watch the video?" She asks, timidly.

"Shelby I have no doubt that Arin loves you like a sister. If she sees that video she will delete it. I'm not saying she won't tease us and give us shit, but that woman would never hurt you." I try to reassure her.

Reaching her hand up, she lays it on my face, "What happens now?"

"That is completely up to you. I want more. More of you. More of this. More of us. But, I won't push you past what you're ready for," I answer.

"Glitch, will you stay? Please, I don't know that I'm ready for more but I don't want to be alone," She begs.

"I'm here," I tell her. "I need to use your bathroom to clean up a bit. I'll be right back."

"There are some men's clothes in a box in the living room if you need them. I think they were Taylor's or Atka's. Arin was supposed to come get them but she forgot."

Reluctantly leaving her side, I find a pair of gray sweatpants in the box and head for the bathroom. After cleaning myself up, I find Shelby sound asleep.

Slipping back out of the room, I make sure everything is locked up before I climb into the bed and wrap my arms around her.

Chapter 6

Shelby

Walking up the steps to my apartment, I notice yet another gift waiting for me. Opening the door, I set my purse down before picking up the flowers and heading to the kitchen.

I can't stop the smile that spreads over my face as I grab a vase to put them in. The gifts started arriving the day after Glitch left on business for his club a week ago.

It's hard to believe that we've been seeing each other for a whole month now. I really should thank the girls for pushing me to go on that first date with him. It's been absolutely amazing so far and I can't wait for him to come back.

Setting the new flowers in the middle of the table, I shake my head at his gesture. It's the second vase of flowers and there's been several boxes of chocolate. One box in particular, he had to have gotten flown in as they are from a very special little shop that I love.

When I got them, I wondered for a half a second how in the world he knew they were my favorite but it's really no surprise that he knew. The man seems to know everything without even asking.

Hurrying to my bedroom, I take a quick shower and search through my closet for something truly sexy to wear. Glitch is supposed to be coming back in tonight and he promised he's come straight here.

I got Arin to watch the kids for me so that we would have the whole night to ourselves. Other than the night of our first date, we've not done anything sexual but I have certainly dreamed about it.

There's only so much my own hands can do to give me the feelings that I felt that night. I want the real thing and I plan on having it tonight.

An hour later, I check my dress in the mirror. It's a deep red with spaghetti straps and barely covers my lady bits but I don't care. I'll only be wearing it here in my apartment for hopefully, only a few minutes.

Grabbing the red stilettos to go with it, I slip them on my feet. I'm just looking at the mirror one last time when I hear a familiar roar of a bike.

My heart racing in the chest as nervousness takes over my body as well as the doubts. Grey was nice once too before he turned abusive.

Putting my hand over my chest, I try to control my breathing just as there's a knock at the door. Walking over to it on shaky legs, I open it slowly with a knowing look on my face.

It takes a second for Glitch to realize what I'm wearing and I watch as his eyes scan me from head to toe. The look of hunger that clouds his eyes has my nipples peeking under my dress.

"Um, I really fucking hope you don't think you're going out in public like that." Glitch growls, looking me straight in the eye.

I gulp at first, afraid of his reaction but his look of hunger never wavers, so I decide to push my luck just a little.

"But don't you like it?" I ask in a husky voice, slowly turning and jutting my ass out just enough for his eyes to move there.

"Fuck yeah, I like it." His own voice barely above a whisper.

Seeing that he still hasn't moved further into the apartment, I walk slowly away from the door.

"Won't you come in? You look hungry. I can fix you something." I look back at him shyly.

"So, you're not going out then?" He seems relieved.

"No." I lean against the wall, arching my back and my breasts catch his attention.

"You're about to fall out of your dress." He growls, licking his lips.

"I hope so." I whisper back and his eyes shoot to mine.

"Shelby. This is a dangerous game you're playing." He says through clenched teeth.

Studying his look, I assure myself that this is Glitch. He won't hurt me.

"But don't you want to play?" I whisper, pushing one strap off my shoulder.

I jump a little as he rushes to me and he stops just short of touching me.

"I want you ready for me, Babe." He says softly, reaching out to lift my face to his own.

"I'm ready, Glitch. Please." I press into him and rub my breasts against his chest.

It feels wonderful to feel the friction it creates on my nipples and I moan.

"Fucking hell!" He growls, slamming his mouth to my own.

His arms wrap around me and his hands land on my ass, grabbing hold and lifting me up. I wrap my legs around his waist, rocking my hips into him. My clit throbs, begging for attention. I feel us moving through the apartment but I don't open my eyes until I feel him setting me on my bed.

"You're not wearing anything under that dress." He kneels in front of me and I smile. "Feet on the bed, spread your knees." He demands.

With my heart racing yet again, I do as he asks, opening up my center for his eyes.

"Fuck, that's beautiful. I'm going to taste you, Shelby." He whispers, looking in my eyes.

I feel my center gush and throb with excitement. This is exactly what I've been craving for a month now. His eyes hold mine as he leans in closer. I can feel his hot breath on my clit.

He starts off slow, kissing my thighs until they quiver. I'm breathing hard and he's yet to touch where I've longed for him to be.

Pushing my little dress up further to my waist, he says, "Eyes on me the whole time, Babe. I want to see that beautiful face when I make you come on my tongue."

I watch in fascination as he leans in but my body reacts instantly when his tongue licks up my center. My eyes close, my head is thrown back and a deep groan climbs up my throat.

"Eyes down here!" He demands and I look back down at him as he continues.

It takes all my willpower to keep my eyes focused. I feel my body climbing higher than it's ever been. The second he sucks my clit into his mouth and glides one finger into my slick center, I lose all control of myself as I scream out my release.

My body is still coming down from that climax when I open my eyes and see Glitch stepping out of his jeans. His body is gloriously covered in tattoos but that's not what currently holds my attention.

His cock is jutting out straight and hard in front of him. Seeing where I'm staring, he grabs himself, sliding his hand up and down.

"You don't stop staring at me like that, I'm probably going to shoot my load before I can feel you coming from the inside." He grins, leaning down to his pants pocket he takes out a foil package.

I smile, thanking him for thinking of such things.

"Fuck I love this dress." He says, climbing over me without putting his full weight down.

"Shouldn't I take it off? And the shoes?" I ask, feeling shy once again.

"Hell no! From now on, anytime you wear this thing, I'll always know how it felt to be as close to you as two people can get." He whispers.

Ripping the foil open, he slides on the condom but he doesn't push his way in right away. Instead, he starts kissing my neck, working his way down to my breasts, pulling them out of the dress.

With his tongue swirling around my nipples, I feel the hardness of him against my center as he slides back and forth, coating himself with my wetness.

Every pump of his hips hits my clit and I begin to push into him with my own. Working his way back up to my lips, he takes my mouth in a deep kiss just as his cock glides itself into me.

I feel so full with him but it feels so good that I can feel my muscles throb on the inside, begging for him to move.

I'm about to break the kiss and beg if I have to but he begins a slow rhythm of sliding almost completely out and back in. Needing more, I throw my hips up just as he slides back in and his cock hits something deep inside that has me moaning yet again.

He must take it as a clue when he slides out and back in at a harder pace. Breaking the kiss, he pumps faster and I wrap my legs around his waist.

A few minutes later, I'm once again screaming out my release and he follows right behind me.

Glitch

After cleaning myself up and helping Shelby take off the dress, I climb back into bed with her, pulling her into my side.

"This was nice. I missed you." I whisper into her hair.

"I missed you too apparently." She giggles.

"I can tell." I chuckle. "How was your week?"

"It was pretty amazing." She snuggles closer.

"Amazing, huh? Why was it so amazing?" Thinking to myself that I may have to kick someone's ass if they are the reason she thinks it was amazing.

"Well, it was the same as any other week. Except for the gifts. Thank you by the way. And how exactly did you know what my favorite chocolates were?" She looks up at my face.

Keeping my confusion to myself, I look back at her. "Hm. My little secret. So tell me, how many gifts did you get?"

"You should know, you sent them." She laughs, poking me in the ribs.

"I know but I want to make sure they sent everything." I comment.

"Six. The last one is sitting on the kitchen table. The flowers are beautiful by the way." She leans up, kissing me on the cheek.

Kissing her back, I snuggle her closer to my side as my mind races with what to do with this information. Her little gifts weren't sent by me and no one in the club would dare step across the line.

"Will you stay tonight? The kids are with Arin until tomorrow." She asks while yawning.

"I have no intention of leaving you tonight. Get some rest." I kiss her head once more as she lays it on my chest.

I wait until she's completely asleep before I slip out of the bed and head to the kitchen.

Seeing the vase of flowers on the table, I narrow my eyes at them. There wasn't any kind of card or note left with the gifts.

Searching the cabinets in the kitchen, I find the remaining chocolates from the box she received yesterday.

Opening the package, I look the pieces over carefully to ensure there wasn't anything added to them although if there had been, Shelby probably would already be dead.

Dialing Eagle's number, I step outside on the first step so that I don't wake up Shelby sleeping in the bedroom.

It takes several rings before he picks up the phone.

"Fucking hell, Glitch. This had better be a fucking emergency waking me up at this hour!" He growls through the phone.

"It is." I answer.

"What's the matter?" His voice instantly becoming serious.

I quickly tell him about all the mystery gifts that Shelby has received this past week and how she thought they were from me.

She still believes that.

"Can we organize a few of the brothers to help watch her and the kids when I can't?" I ask.

"You already know the answer to that. We should probably meet with Atka and Taylor, let them know what's going on."

"They might tell her and I'd rather she didn't know. Not now that she's trying so hard to not let her past bother her so much. Hell, she's just now starting to be okay with the kids staying the night with Arin."

"They won't tell her, that I know for a fact."

"How do you know that? They aren't part of the club. Not really." I ask.

"Because I have a secret weapon." He laughs through the phone. "My sweet sister in law who happens to consider Shelby her sister."

"Fuck, Brother, you get too much glee from using your sister in law against your brother." I laugh.

"I never thought I'd enjoy it so much, personally, but I fucking love that woman! But hey, I'll take care of everything. You staying there tonight?"

"Yeah."

"Good. When we leave in the morning, there'll be a brother parked within sight. We'll go over some more details later. I need my beauty sleep." As he says the last part, I hear a woman giggle and I just shake my head as I hang up the phone.

There's no one in our club more of a player than Eagle. Not even Mac or Sticks can match him when it comes to getting women. While the rest of us may occasionally go back for seconds with a woman, Eagle absolutely never does.

They get his attention for only a few hours before he leaves them without a backwards glance.

I've wondered before what in his past has him so against settling with just one but I keep my thoughts to myself. Eagle keeps his own council. I'm not sure he's really close to anyone. Not even his brother.

Walking back inside, I lock back up and go back to the kitchen for a drink of water before heading back to bed.

Slipping back under the covers, I pull my sleeping beauty up against me once more and fall asleep with her ass pressed into my hips.

Chapter 7

Shelby

I kind of feel bad for Arin. She invited me here to take care of her kids and she's been taking care of mine. Not like an everyday thing, and I keep her kids when the shop is open or Taylor has to work. But, ever since Glitch got back from that trip with the club last month, Arin takes Bry and Dyna on my days off.

She says it's not a big deal, two or four kids, makes no difference. Even Cass has taken them a couple of times. Glitch has been here every day getting to know the kids and spending time with us.

When the kids are around, he keeps everything pg, but the minute they are out of sight he is on me like white on rice. I don't mind one little bit. Our sexscapades are beyond anything I could have imagined.

It's not just the sex that turns me on though. It's the little things like the gifts I still receive almost every day. The way he talks to my son, and listens to what Bry has to say.

Last week he fell asleep on the couch watching Frozen with Dyna. I had gone to help Bryson with his bath and when I was finished, I found Glitch and Dyna cuddled together with her little head drooling on his chest.

He's taken the kids to the park a few times, suggesting I take a bath or drink a glass of wine.

The first time he did it, I was totally panicking while they were gone but when they stumbled back in two hours later laughing and exhausted I wondered why I even worried.

Tonight I've got all the kids, Olivia, Aiden, Liza and my own. Glitch is here, he's been building Lego fortes with Bry and Aiden while the girls are watching Moana and I'm cooking dinner.

Arin, Cass, and Mika are down at the shop working. Mika is technically not supposed to be working anymore but she insists on being at the shop while Taylor and Atka are away on an overnight trip. Jake has a late class at the gym, he does that sometimes for people that work during the day.

I'm pulling a tray out of the oven when a sudden pounding on my door makes me jump, sending tater tots flying all over the kitchen.

"Shelby! Shelby, open the door." Arin's voice calls out.

"Dammit Woman! You nearly gave me a heart attack." I say letting her in.

I don't notice Glitch is right behind me until I step back into him. "Why are you pounding on the door like a mad woman?" He demands.

After catching her breath, Arin tells us "Mika is in labor."

"Why are you here, then?" I ask. "We have a plan in place. All you had to do was text me."

"I wanted to see Aiden and Olivia before they went to bed." she answers.

After hugging and kissing her kids, Arin leaves but tells me that Cass will be up in a minute. They didn't want to leave Mika alone.

When Cass comes to the door she looks mad instead of happy. "That bitch has been having contractions all day but does she tell anyone? No, she waits until her water breaks and says she was trying to hold the baby in until Atka gets back!" She grumbles.

She scoops Liza up and blows raspberries on her belly. "You, be a good girl until Daddy gets here." She coos at her daughter, then gives her kisses before putting her back down.

"Jake shouldn't be too much longer. His class has about thirty minutes left." She tells me on her way out the door.

As I watch her go down the stairs, Glitch asks me "What are you waiting for?"

"Huh?"

"Go with them." He says.

"I can't, the kids." I remind him.

"The kids are with me and Jake will be here soon. I got this. Hurry before they leave without you."

I look from him to the kids hesitating. If it was just my kids I'd be out the door already. I trust this man with my life, but Arin and Cass might not be okay with it.

He must be reading my mind because he tells me to run down there and ask them. "Hurry." He says but I still hold back.

"What if they don't want me there?" I question.

"I have heard every single one of those women refer to you as their sister. Now go be with them." He pushes me out the door and closes it behind me.

When I turn the corner of the building I find Cass and Mika in the car but no sign of Arin. "Where's Arin?" I ask through the open window.

"Trying to get rid of an asshole," Mika calmly answers.

Turning to look in the shop window I see Arin arguing with a man. Her face is red and her arms are flailing around to make her point.

The man is twice her size but Arin isn't backing down. I'm not as brave as her but I'm not going to let anyone hurt my family either. So I march inside. I'm just in time to hear Arin yell, "If you ever come back to my shop, I'm going to tattoo a two-inch penis on your ass."

"I paid for your time! You can't leave me with half of a fucking tiger!" he yells back.

"I gave you your money back and told you I would finish it FREE OF CHARGE!!" she rebuts.

"In the meantime, I have half of a fucking tiger!"

I can see this isn't getting anywhere so I interrupt. "Arin you gotta go."

"I know," she snaps, throwing her hands up in the air. "But this asshole won't leave my shop so I can lock up."

"Hey Mister," I address him. "You see that woman that's in labor, out there waiting for her sister?"

"Yes, so what? I want my piece finished." He responds.

"Well her brother is the President of the Midnight Sons and if she has that baby in the car, he's going to kick your ass." I tell him.

Watching the color drain from his face is probably one of the funniest things I've ever seen. He looks between us as if trying to determine if I'm telling the truth, then runs out of the shop like his ass is on fire.

Helping her lock up, Arin asks why I'm not upstairs and I explain that Glitch offered to watch the kids if that was alright with her and Cass. Before she even has a chance to answer, Cass yells "Get your asses in the car!"

Three hours later, I'm sitting in the family waiting room when a commotion from the hall gets my attention. When I go to check it out, because I'm nosy of course, I see Eagle at the nurses station with ten of his club members.

"My sister is in labor." He tells her.

She looks at all the guys in disbelief and I think she's going to send them away so I step forward.

"Eagle," I call out. "In here."

Once they all file in, I explain. "They won't allow more than two in the room with her at a time. So me, Arin and Cass have been switching out."

Most of the guys get comfortable but Eagle is pacing and texting on his phone. Watching him circle the room is making me dizzy so I offer to go get coffee for everyone.

Sticks volunteers to help and when we return both Arin and Cass are in the waiting room.

Seeing all the guys still in the room I ask, "Who's with Mika?"

"We've been replaced," Arin pouts.

"Taylor and Atka are with her now," Cass finishes before we are interrupted by a nurse.

"Mrs. Burns," she calls out. "Arin Burns."

"That's me," Arin answers as she steps forward. "Is everything okay? Is my sister alright?"

"Your sister is fine but, um, your husband passed out." the nurse answers.

The guys all start laughing but Arin spins on them, "That is his baby sister in there squeezing a watermelon out of her vagina! Any of you give him shit and I'll knee each and every one of you fuckers right in the nuts!"

Every man in the room cups himself and groans as Arin walks out behind the nurse.

"Don't worry little guy, I'll protect you." Sticks mumbles next to me.

"Sticks?" I question. "Are you talking to your penis?"

A few minutes later Arin returns with a very pale Taylor leaning heavily on her. Neither of them sit down, they stand silently at the entrance.

You can hear a pin drop and the room goes so completely silent.

"Ahnah Claire Heartsong weighs six pounds eleven ounces." Taylor finally announces with a big smile.

Glitch

The night Mika gave birth to Ahnah and I volunteered to stay with the kids, honestly scared the shit out of me.

I was getting closer to Bryson and Dyna, spending a lot of time with them but with Olivia, Liza and Aiden in the mix, it was hectic until Jake arrived and stayed to help me.

I notice that Bryson is quieter than usual. He started out real quiet but he has been opening up the last few weeks. I need to fix this before he reverts back to that scared little boy I first met.

Jake and I decide the best way to tackle bedtime with five kids under six years old is to spread blankets on the floor and let them 'camp out' with a movie.

Once everyone is settled down I ask Bry to help me get the pillows off his bed. Once we are in his room, I sit him down.

"Bry, what's wrong?" I ask him gently.

To my shock he starts crying, "Is Uncle Atka going to be mean to the baby?"

"What!?" I'm shocked and don't know how to answer at first. Giving myself a moment to think, I run my hands through my hair.

"Daddies are mean." He goes on to inform me. I take a deep breath.

"No Bryson, not all daddies are mean." I can't exactly tell a five-year-old that his dad is just an asshole. "Have you ever seen Taylor be mean to Aunt Arin? Olivia or Aiden?"

"No, Uncle Taylor saved us! He took us away from my bad daddy." It's almost adorable the way he defends Taylor.

"Did you know that Taylor is Mika's big brother?" I ask him.

"Uh-huh." He nods his head.

"Well, it's a big brother's job to protect his little sister. If Atka ever even thinks about hurting Mika or the baby, Uncle Taylor will keep them safe."

"Is Glitch your real name? It's a weird name." His sudden change of subject makes my head spin but I'm happy for the reprieve.

"No," I laugh. "My real name is Adam. Do you know what a glitch is?" I ask him.

"No," he answers me.

I go on to explain, "A glitch is a mistake in a game or a computer. When my brothers found out I could fix computers they started calling me Glitch, it's a nickname. Like your name is Bryson but the people that love you call you Bry."

"Uncle Glitch?"

"Yes little man," I ask, curious about what he could possibly ask me next.

"Can I go watch the movie now?"

Laughing, I playfully push him towards the door, "Get outta here."

I'm awakened by the sound of a door opening just before sunrise, I open my eyes to see Shelby and Cass attempting to tiptoe through the living room. The only thing that stops me from laughing out loud when Cass trips over Jake's legs is knowing it would wake the kids.

"I'm going to take Jake and Liza home." She tells Shelby. "Arin will probably close the shop for a couple of days. Get some sleep and we'll call you later."

After Cass, Jake, and Liza leave, Shelby waves her hand to signal me into the kitchen. She heads straight for the coffee maker but finds it already prepared.

"Oh Thank God," She sighs while pouring herself a cup.

I wrap my arms around her from behind and she leans back into me. "Where is Taylor and Arin?" I ask, keeping my voice low so I don't wake the kids.

"They had to stick around. Taylor passed out in the delivery room, so the doctor is making sure his blood pressure - blood sugar and all that stuff is where it's supposed to be." She answers.

"Taylor passed out? But he was in the delivery room with Arin when Aiden and Olivia were born." I'm shocked.

"Apparently it's not the same when the woman squeezing a new life out of her hoo-ha is your baby sister." Shelby laughs and explains, "They didn't plan for him to be in there but by the time they got back from Thorne Bay everything was moving fast."

"You probably won't have to keep Aiden and Olivia for a few weeks," I tell her and she looks at me confused.

"Why? Mika had a baby, not Arin." She asks.

"Has Mika ever told you about her past?" I need to know how much she knows. If Mika hasn't said anything then it's not my story to share.

"I know she was kidnapped as a kid and only found Taylor a few years ago, if that's what you mean."

"She was kidnapped from the hospital as a baby by one of the nurses. Taylor witnessed it but he was too young to understand what was happening. He has always blamed himself."

"Oh," is all she has a chance to say before a gentle tapping comes from the door. I let her out of my arms to answer it.

Inviting Arin and Taylor into the kitchen, she pours them each a cup of coffee. Arin looks exhausted but Taylor looks pissed off, judging by the scowl on his face.

"What's wrong old man? I didn't think I'd see your face outside of the hospital for a few days." I ask him.

Unexpectedly it's Arin who answers while laughing, "I'm not sure who is worse, Taylor or Eagle. Taylor threatening every person in the maternity ward or Eagle stationing a Midnight Son at every entrance and exit."

Taylor just growls and drinks his coffee.

Arin continues, "I had to drag him out of there. Ahnah Claire is going to be the most spoiled Princess. I pity the boys when she gets older."

Shelby gathers up Olivia and Aiden's things, while Taylor and Arin each pick up a kid and carry them out. Taking the backpack from Shelby, I let her know I'll be right back and follow them down to help get the kids loaded.

Standing on the sidewalk watching them drive off, something flashes across the street. There are two buildings, one is a quilting store and the other is a clothing store. Between the buildings is a small gap. The gap is just big enough for a person to walk through.

Looking up at Shelby's door, I decide to check it out. We still haven't been able to track down Porter. The street lights here are well lit but the sun hasn't come up yet and I'm unarmed.

I keep my piece locked up when I'm around the kids. So I walk like I'm going back upstairs then slip behind the building to where my bike is parked. Lifting the seat to access my microsafe, I make sure no one is around before I unlock it and pull out my Smith & Wesson M&P.

Instead of going back the way I came from, I slip around a couple of buildings and approach the gap from the opposite side. If there is someone there, they won't see me coming.

Crouching down as low to the ground as possible with my gun in my hand, I slip into the gap. The front is lit up by the street lights but it gets darker as I go further back. Almost to where I think should be the back of the buildings a sudden noise makes me jump to attention, pointing my gun at the sound.

Keeping my gun up and aiming to the sound I quietly back up towards the light. I don't want to shoot some random homeless person so I don't have my finger on the trigger but I am prepared to shoot if I have to. When suddenly a hissing noise echoes through the gap and a cat screeches past me.

Letting out a breath, I didn't realize I was holding, I slip my gun into the pocket of my cut. The flash I saw must have been light reflecting off the cat's eyes. Looking around once more, I notice movement under a piece of cardboard so I flip it over and find a kitten.

It doesn't appear to be much older than six weeks, and knowing there is a cold front coming in the next few days, I can't leave the little guy out here. Mama cat must have been protecting her baby. I'll bring back some cat food for her later, maybe I can catch her and take them both to the shelter.

Greyson

That fucking cunt almost caught me! Shelby is going to pay for stealing my princess and spreading her fucking legs for that piece of shit in leather. I gave her everything a woman could fucking want! How does she repay me, by being a two-timing whore! Maybe I'll fuck her before I kill the bitch, remind her what a real man feels like between her thighs.

The bitch never could do anything except lay there like a slab of pork while I rutted into her. The only good thing about sex with that slut was her tight pussy!

Her dad fired me when he saw me looking at his precious daughter, well look at me now asshole! You're dead and I fucked your angel. She thinks she can take away everything I've worked for just because that little bastard got an owie!

I'll give him a fucking owie when I break every bone in his body and bury him. All I have to do is keep him alive long enough to claim her inheritance, then it's bye bye Bryson. My precious might be sad that her brother and her mommy are gone but I'll make it up to her.

Chapter 8

Shelby

I'm going stir crazy! Glitch was right about Taylor going into overprotective Daddy mode. For the last two weeks, Taylor has taken time off and stayed with his kids so it's just been me and my kids.

But, Every time I try to leave the apartment, Glitch is there standing in my way with some excuse why I shouldn't go out. "It's going to rain," he says. "It's too cold to take the kids out," He tells me.

If I need groceries, he insists on going for me. I'm sick and tired of it! I let one man control me and he turned out to be an abusive douche. I'll never let another man do that shit to me.

I haven't been feeling good for two weeks now and everything is getting on my damn nerves. Holding back has only made me even more aggravated but I won't confront him in front of my kids, they've seen enough shit from their dad to last a lifetime.

Arin is probably getting sick of me calling her and venting about Glitch. The first time I called her, she laughed!

"It's the baby," she explained. "Everyone of the Midnight Sons plus Atka and Taylor have gone off the deep end since Ahnah was born."

She told me to wait it out, but how long should I wait this shit out. I'm done. I'm sending the kids to Arin's house tonight and I'm going to confront him. But first, I need to run to the bathroom and puke my guts out.

That's where Glitch finds me, bent over the toilet bowl. He pulls my hair back and waits until I'm finished before handing me my toothbrush and a glass of water.

"Are you okay?" He asks me.

"Seriously?" I snap, "Am I okay? Do I look okay?" I brush my teeth and stomp off to my bedroom, slamming the door behind me. I know the kids are safe with him and I'm exhausted from vomiting, so I curl up on my bed and fall asleep.

Glitch

"Fuck!" I yell at the empty bathroom. Shelby has been sick for the last couple of days and I've been an asshole. Maybe she's allergic to cats? When I brought the kitten back I never thought she would keep it. But the minute she set eyes on the little orange and white fluffball, she claimed it, naming it George.

I know I'm being an asshole but ever since I saw that flash in the gap across the street, I've been on edge. None of my sources can find Greyson Porter. It's like he vanished off the face of the Earth but I know better. Men like him can't hide for long.

Waiting a few minutes to follow her, I find Shelby sound asleep. So I gently close the door and head for the kitchen. I'm not a cook but I can make some basic stuff. Preparing lunch of grilled cheese and tomato soup for the kids keeps me occupied for a little bit.

After they eat and take a nap, I decide to take them to the park so she can rest. The sun is shining but it's a little chilly outside, winter isn't far away so this might be one of the last days for them to get out.

First I have to wake her up and let her know we're going. If she wakes up to an empty apartment she's going to freak out.

"Shelby," I nudge her shoulder gently.

"Hmm?"

"I'm going to take the kids to the park so you can rest." I whisper.

"Okay," She mumbles before rolling over.

Getting a two year old ready to go out isn't as easy as I thought it would be, thankfully Bryson helps. I leave a note on the fridge as back up in case she wasn't awake enough to be aware of our conversation.

When we arrive at the park I notice that Arin and Taylor had the same idea. Taylor and I stay close to the monkey bars watching over Olivia and Bryson, while Arin takes the little ones over to the swings.

My attention is drawn to the little ones an hour later when I hear Dyna squealing and laughing. I look over and see her running towards me with Arin and Aiden chasing her. She has her arms held out to me and she's shouting, "Dada Dada."

I swear to God, the Earth and the moon, my heart melts into a puddle of goo. "I'll save you from the wild Aunty!" I blurt out, scooping her into my arms and swinging her around.

On the second spin, I notice someone watching. He has long hair and a wild dirty beard so I can't make out his face. He's hunched over making it impossible to guess his height but he has eyes on the kids and it's creepy.

Calling Taylor closer I ask him, "Did you walk or do you have a car here? Laugh like I said something funny."

Taylor lets out a laugh, catching on fast. "We walked, why?"

"There is someone watching the kids. I don't recognize him and he's not one of my brothers." I tell him.

"We'll walk back with you, get Shelby's kids upstairs. I'll have Arin and my kids go into the shop. While I call Eagle." Taylor says, while gathering up his family.

"Time to go." I call out. The kids aren't happy about it but then I remind Bryson that he's going to spend the night at Olivia's house and suddenly he's eager to go.

Taking one last look around, the man I saw is no longer in sight.

Shelby

Waking up to a quiet apartment is so rare that I take advantage of every moment. I'm upset that the Glitch took the kids to the park when he has been blocking me from taking them, but grateful for the peace and quiet.

I'm vacuuming when they get back so I don't hear the door open. It isn't until little arms wrap around my legs that I know my reprieve is over.

"Mommy! Dyna called Glitch, Dada!" Bry is quick to tell me.

I pull her into my arms and smooch her, "Did my girl learn a new word?"

"Da da, Da da." She repeats and leans away reaching for Glitch.

Stunned, I let her go to him and walk out of the room. So far, she has only said Mama and she calls Bry "bye bye" so a new word is a big deal. A few minutes later as I pack the kid's overnight bags, Glitch joins me. Leaning against the doorway to their room he says, "I didn't teach her that. I swear."

"It's ok," I tell him. "Babies get confused."

Trying to brush it off for now. This development is just going to make our discussion later more difficult. With my back to him, I place my hand on my belly. It's already going to be hard enough to break up with him.

"Taylor and Arin were at the park with us. Arin has their kids downstairs and Taylor went to get the car." He continues.

"But they only live like two blocks away?" I ask, confused.

"I don't know. Maybe he's taking them out for ice cream or something." Glitch shrugs his shoulders.

Letting out a sigh, just another thing to confirm I'm making the right decision. He must think I'm stupid if he thinks I don't know something is going on.

When Taylor knocks on the door, I hand him Bryson's bag and watch them walk downstairs. Then I pick up Dyna and her bag but when I get to the door, Glitch holds his hands out for her.

"I got her," I snap. But he persists and I give in just to get it over with.

It doesn't take long before Glitch comes back through the door. He finds me pacing and wringing my hands. When he tries to hug me, I step away.

"What is it, Shelby? Talk to me." He scrunches his face up in confusion, but I don't answer right away.

After a couple of deep breaths, I'm finally able to figure out what I need to say.

"I grew up alone. My parents kept me locked down from as far back as I can remember. I had them and they spoiled me rotten but the only kids I ever saw were the kids of their friends. The only people I interacted with on a daily basis were people approved by them. All because some photographer snuck onto one of Mom's sets and took pictures of me."

"Do you know what that's like to be so completely alone? Then I met Greyson, he swept me off my feet, took me to restaurants and movies. I craved that, seeing real people out in the real world was like a drug and I couldn't get enough of it. It didn't last, as soon as he put a ring on my finger, I was once again locked up in a prison. Yeah it was a beautiful prison but he wouldn't even let me go grocery shopping. He claimed it was all for my protection, then the kids came along and it was to protect them."

Pausing to take a deep breath, Glitch tries to say something but I hold my hand up to stop him. "I'm not done."

"The only thing I needed protection from was him and now you are doing the same thing."

"What? No!" He blurts out.

"Glitch, I never asked you to move in. You just never left and I didn't say anything. Everytime I try to go somewhere or do something, you have a reason why I can't. I refuse to let you or anyone else control me ever again." I start crying.

"What are you saying?" Glitch asks.

"I want you to leave please." I answer.

"I'm trying to keep you safe. Greyson is out there and nobody can find him." That's when I completely lose it and scream at him.

"Jake taught me how to defend myself and Arin taught me how to use a gun! I refuse to be a prisoner ever again!" I shout.

"When did Arin teach you to shoot?" Glitch questions me.

"Before I left California. She volunteered to teach a class at the women's shelter. The point is I have a gun and know how to use it. I don't need a man to protect me, to stand in front of me. What I need is someone to stand by my side, to be my partner."

"My son needs someone to teach him how to be a good man, and my daughter needs someone to chase off future boyfriends and treat her like a princess. That man can't be you Glitch. Not if you're going to keep stepping in front of me." Instead of waiting for him to respond, I walk out of the room.

Standing in my room with my back against the door, I listen as he moves around for a few minutes and then leaves.

Tears are streaming down my face as I go back out to make sure everything is locked up.

After spending the night crying on the couch, I get up determined not to let Bry and Dyna see what a mess I am. First stop is the shower, well second stop is the shower. The first stop ends up being the toilet bowl to puke my guts out, again.

It's only a few minutes after my shower when Arin arrives with my babies. They charge in, full of energy and are ready to start the day. I honestly just want to climb into my bed for the next week but I know that won't happen.

Arin watches as I pull out some toys for Dyna to play with and Bryson takes his bag to his room. He comes running back out, "Mama where is Glitch? I gotta tell him all about the awesome car movie I watched with Uncle Taylor."

"Glitch had to go to work." I tell him.

"When will he be back?" Bry wants to know.

"I don't know baby, he has to do grown-up stuff."

"I'm gonna go play in my room." He sadly walks away, breaking my heart all over again.

Bryson

When we moved here, Mommy was happy but now she's sad again. She doesn't see me peeking out of my bedroom door after Aunt Arin leaves. I'm being real quiet, did something happen to Glitch? I wanted him to be my Daddy, he promised he wouldn't ever hurt Mommy but she's crying.

Now I don't know if I should ask him or not. Mommy doesn't have owies like Daddy used to give her when he hit her. She's sad and I don't know what would make her sad. I've been good and I've been helping take care of Dyna like a good big brother.

When Mommy doesn't do nothing except watch sissy and cry, I decide to play with my toys. That's what I'm doing when Mommy decides to take us to Stella's. We love Stella's, we get to eat and play and if there is other kids there it's even more fun.

Mommy carries Dyna cause she's little but I'm a big kid so I can walk as long as I hold her hand. It's cold outside and there is snowflakes falling. It's the prettiest thing I've ever seen. We didn't get snow at my old house.

I can barely wait to play in it, Olivia says when there's lots of snow we can build a snowman. Like the one in the movie Frozen that Dyna loves to watch. I don't like it cause there is kissing and I would never kiss a girl.

Chicken nuggets and french fries is my favorite food. Mommy gets that for both of us, but she doesn't get nothing for herself.

"Mommy are you gonna eat?" I asks her.

"No baby, my tummy doesn't feel good." She answers.

I heard mommy throwing up yesterday, and that's even more gross than girls. Maybe Mommy is just sad because she's sick. After we eat Mommy lets us play.

I'm on the slide when I see Mommy holding her tummy and talking to a lady. The lady's little boy was at Mama Lou's, when we picked up Olivia one day. Then Mommy goes to the bathroom real fast.

When I get down the slide Mommy isn't back yet, so I go play with Dyna in the ball pit. Ball pits are for babies but I gotta watch her, it's my job.

I'm not watching nobody but my sister, so when someone puts his hand on my shoulder I get scared. Then I hear daddy's voice, "Bryson help your sister put her coat and shoes back on."

"You...you're not sposed to be here." I tell him.

He squishes my shoulder real hard and tells me I better listen. That's when the lady walks over.

"Who are you?" she asks Daddy.

"I'm their father. Their mother is sick so I came to take them home." He answers her, real nice.

The lady doesn't look like she believes him, so she asks me, "Is this man your Daddy?"

My arm hurts, "Yes ma'am" I answer cause I know Daddy will hurt me more if I don't.

Chapter 9

Shelby

Uhg! I hate vomiting, especially in public bathrooms. People look at you as if you've got the plague. The timing and location was bad but thankfully Cora Jean, one of mom's that used to take her kids to Mama Lou's is here with her son.

When the urge to vomit hits me so bad that I can't put it off, Asking Cora Jean to keep an eye on the kids for me. I try to be quick but it's not like I can control it.

After splashing some water on my face, I return to the play area only to find it empty. Cora Jean is helping her son put his shoes back on but my kids are nowhere in sight.

"Cora! Where are they?" I practically shout in her face.

"They left with their Dad, he said he was taking you home," She replies. "Did I do something wrong? The little boy confirmed that he was their father."

Running as fast as I can, I head straight for the apartment with hope that's where the kids will be.

Tears fall from my eyes uncontrollably and people passing me on the sidewalks stop to stare as I race by.

I just keep repeating to myself that my babies are okay. That, maybe it's not really Grey that has them but maybe one of the guys from the club.

As I round the corner, I spot the stairs to my apartment above the shop. I try to take the stairs two at a time, slipping once and bouncing my knee off the step.

Pain shoots through my leg and a fast glance tells me it's bleeding but I continue up the stairs quickly, throwing the door open.

It's then I realize it wasn't locked but I rush through the apartment, looking in every small room for a sign of my babies.

Walking back to the kitchen on wobbly legs, I see through my tears enough to notice a note on the kitchen table.

Snatching it up, I wipe my eyes, trying to clear them.

My Beautiful Wife,

You're just as beautiful today as you were when we first started dating. I was never planning to actually marry you though, no matter how beautiful you were. Did you know that? Did you know that I actually hated having to touch you? But I started liking the idea of you giving me a little girl so I continued fucking that pussy of yours. You had to be a bitch though and pop out that monster of a boy. I should have killed him in his crib. The only reason I didn't was because he kept you out of my hair for a while. You did finally give me my sweet little girl though but only because I switched out your birth control pills with sugar tablets. I found it highly entertaining to watch you wonder why you were gaining so much weight the months before you got pregnant again. You're lucky it was a girl that time. My sweet Dyna. She's why I'm here. Mostly. If you want this brat of a son to see another birthday, you'll meet me at the Kincaid Park. Alone Wife. If not, I'll slit his fucking throat before you even know where he's at.

Signed,

Grey

My hand goes to my throat, holding in a scream. This bastard is so full of himself, he actually wrote this note on his own office letterhead.

The room starts to spin and I grab hold of the table, squeezing my eyes shut. My rapid breathing is causing a panic attack.

If I don't slow down, I'll pass out and there's no time to waste. He has my kids.

I've always known he hated having a son although I chose not to acknowledge it.

How can a man hate having a little boy? Not to mention his admission to fucking with my birth control.

Only a crazy person would do such a thing.

Grabbing my purse, I rush back out the door. Maybe I can find a cab a few streets over that can get me to Kincaid park quickly.

Before he does something to my sweet little boy.

The thought has my eyes clouding over again and I trip the last few steps down the stairs.

I'm almost to the street and about to cross when I feel a hand on my arm.

"Shelby! What's going on?" Cass demands, spinning me to look at her.

I open my mouth but nothing comes out and she drags me toward the front door of the shop, pushing me inside.

Guiding me to a chair, she pushes me to sit.

"Take a breath and tell me what's going on!" She puts her hands on her hips, looking me over.

She must notice the letter clinched in my hand as she snatches it away and begins to read.

"Oh hell no!" She exclaims and I stand back up.

"I've got to go. He's going to hurt my babies. Oh my sweet babies!" I start crying again, unable to see through the tears and she sets me back into the chair behind me.

"Don't worry. We'll get them back. Stay right here, let me call the other girls." She runs over the desk, grabbing her phone.

I cry all through her conversation and have no idea who exactly she called. By the time she comes back to me, I'm no longer in control of myself at all.

Cass

I watch as Shelby breaks down completely sitting across the room. Mika's phone rings several times before she answers.

"Bitch, I was finally sleeping!" Mika starts to complain.

"We have a major fucking problem." I tell her.

"Do I hear someone crying? Who's fucking crying?" Mika demands.

"Shelby. Someone, actually not just someone but her Ex has taken the kids!"

"You know for a fact it was him? He's here?" She asks just as I hear Atka in the background asking who's here.

"It was him, the note he left for her in the apartment confirms it. The fucker wrote it on his own fucking office letterhead!" I growl, glancing back at Shelby who hasn't moved or stopped crying.

"Have you called anyone else?" Mika asks.

"No. You were my first call but I should probably call Glitch."

"You call Glitch, I'll call everyone else." She says quickly, hanging up.

Immediately dialing Glitch's number, it rings for only a second before he answers.

"Glitch, there's a problem. Get to the shop immediately." I say, hanging up quickly before he can demand answers. I'd rather not have to explain a billion times over the phone. I've got to take care of one of my sisters.

Going to the break room quickly, I grab a washcloth soaking it in cold water and head back to Shelby.

"Shelby, look up for me sweetie. You've got to stop this fucking insane crying now." I wait for several long minutes. "Shelby!" I yell and she looks up at me.

"Let's wash your face and stop crying now. Help is coming and it's best if they can comprehend what you are saying. Okay?" I ask and she shakes her head without actually answering but the crazy crying has stopped.

Just as I'm finishing wiping her face, we hear vehicles and bikes pulling into the parking lot out back. I sigh with relief that reinforcements have arrived.

Glitch

Getting to the Poison Pen shop, I rush through the doors, searching for Shelby. When our eyes meet, she runs into my arms, tears streaming down her beautiful face.

"It's okay, Babe. We'll find them." I say into her hair, breathing in her fresh scent.

"He left this note for her in the apartment upstairs." Taylor says, handing me a piece of paper.

My fist clenches when I notice the fucker wrote it on his own fucking letterhead. He's truly fucked in the head.

"Well, obviously she's not going there alone!" I huff out.

"I have to! He says he'll kill Bryson. My sweet little Bry!" She breaks down once again.

"Now look at what you did!" Cass shoves me in the shoulder as the other girls gather around Shelby.

"I need to call Eagle." I say to no one in particular.

"I already did. He's on the way with several of the guys." Atka answers.

As I watch the other girls take care of mine, my mind races with thoughts of Bryson being so scared of the man who created him. A man that seems to truly hate him for no other reason than being a boy.

Remembering what all was in the letter, I think about Kincaid park.

I've been there several times. It's not normally packed with people. There's so many damn trees, a person could hide forever out there.

Or sneak up on someone.

As a plan begins to form in my mind, I make my way to the back door. Just as I open the door to step out, I'm stopped by Atka's voice.

"Where are you going?" He demands.

"I can't sit here and do nothing. I'm the VP of the club. I can at least scope out the park and provide intel directly to Eagle." I say in a hushed tone.

"You're going to call him then?" He asks with a raised brow.

"Of course. He's my Prez." I growl, walking quickly to my bike.

It takes nearly forty minutes to get to the park because of all the traffic.

Finding the main entrance, I pass it up, remembering another tiny path not far down that leads directly into the park.

Most tourists never find this entrance, only locals really know about it but I cut my engine off just inside the trees just in case.

Silently making my way through the trees, I try my best to not make a lot of noise with my boots even though it's bear season.

Be my luck I'd spook a bear and get mauled to death. That would be one hell of a glitch.

Suddenly, a figure emerged from the shadows of the trees. A malicious grin etched on his face.

"Glitch," Grey sneered, his voice laced with a cruel satisfaction. "I must admit, I didn't expect you to come searching for them. How noble. You must really love that bitch."

I clenched my fists, my body tense with a mix of anxiety and anger.

"Where are the kids, Grey?" I demanded. "What have you done with them?"

Grey's laughter pierced the air, echoing around the desolate park. "You think you can outsmart me, Glitch? You're just a pawn in this game. The kids are safe, for now. But you... you're going to pay for meddling in my affairs. For fucking my wife."

My mind raced, searching for a plan. I had to find a way to turn the tables on him. My eyes darted around, looking for any advantage I could seize.

As I contemplated my next move, a surge of memories flooded my mind—memories of the kids, their laughter, and the love they had shown me.

I couldn't let them down. I couldn't let this fucker win.

Taking a deep breath, I locked eyes with Grey, my voice steady and resolute. "I won't let you get away with this. Not with the kids. They deserve better than you, and I'll do whatever it takes to bring them back safely."

Grey's expression hardened, his grip tightening on something hidden beneath his coat.

I braced myself for what was about to come, but deep down, I knew that I would fight until my last breath to protect those kids. They were family. MY family.

I rush forward, hoping to catch him off guard but it doesn't work as he shoots me with what was under his coat.

My body falls face first as it feels like I'm being hit by a thousand lightning bolts.

My teeth grind together as I try to fight it but it's too much. The world around me goes completely dark.

Chapter 10

Shelby

"WAIT! WAIT! WAIT!" Everyone keeps telling me to wait and let them create a plan. These are my kids but they are talking around me as if I don't matter.

Eagle, Atka and Taylor are saying to wait for Glitch to check in. Arin, Cass and Mika want to charge in and take him down. They are arguing over how to do it, when my phone rings.

It's an unknown number and nobody hears it but me because they are all talking over each other. Finally I've had enough, "SHUT UP!" I shout.

The only sound now is my phone still ringing. I reach to answer it, but Taylor puts his hand over mine. "Put it on speaker phone." He tells me.

I nod my head and hit the answer button.

A woman's voice says, "Hello."

"Can I help you?" I ask.

"My name is Belinda Steel. I work for a Nanny agency in Anchorage, Alaska." She answers.

"Miss Steel, I don't need a nanny and I'm in the middle of something so please get to your point." I demand running out of patience.

"I'm sorry ma'am. I'm trying to reach the mother of Bryson and Dyna Porter."

"That's me!" I shout, grabbing my phone tighter.

"The agency called me this morning about an emergency placement. Mister Porter gave my boss a sob story about his wife being deceased and he needed someone fast that would be willing to temporarily relocate. I met him at the Ballard hotel downtown about an hour ago with the kids and I could tell right away something wasn't right."

Tears are streaming down my face and I'm holding my breath as she continues. "The little girl is real quiet and clinging to her brother. Bryson seemed frightened when they arrived. Mister Porter left the kids here with me saying he had to tie up loose ends and make travel arrangements. As soon as the door closed behind him, Bryson demanded I call his mom. Bryson is one smart little boy, he gave me this phone number and wouldn't stop yelling until I dialed the phone."

I'm speechless, so Taylor jumps in, "Miss Steel, my name is Taylor Burns. I'm the kid's Uncle and I'm a lawyer in Anchorage. You can google my name if that makes you feel better about what I'm going to say." he pauses to make sure she's listening.

"In about twenty minutes a woman is going to knock on your door. She is five foot one inch tall with short dark hair and tattoos. That woman is my wife, her name is Arin and she's going to tell you that kids love liver and onions for dinner. The kids are going to leave with her and you are going to get the hell out of there. Does Greyson know your personal information?"

"No," she answers. "That's one of the things that I thought was unusual. He didn't ask me any questions about myself except my first name. Am I in danger Mr. Burns?"

"I don't believe you are since he doesn't know anything about you. Just do exactly what I've told you." Taylor replies.

"I swear I will." She confirms before the line goes dead.

"Liver and Onions?" I question breaking the silence.

"It was the first thing I could think of, It's not something a person would normally say." Taylor shrugs and we all laugh.

The relief of knowing where my kids are is like someone lifted a fifty-ton weight off my chest and I can breathe again.

I know he means well but when Eagle speaks next I want to scream. "You know it's not over. Getting the kids back is only half of the battle. You have to confront him or he's just going to keep coming back."

"I'm going to take Arin, Atka, and Cass with me to the hotel. Arin and Cass will go to the room for the kids. Atka and I will be back-up. Eagle, can you send a few guys as escorts?" Taylor lays out his plan for getting the kids.

"Why am I not going? I'm their mother!" I demand.

"In case it's a setup." Taylor calmly answers me.

"I'll take Olivia, Aiden and Liza over to the gym they can play in the kid's room." Jake steps up.

"Can you take Mika and Ahnah with you please?" Atka asks. "I would feel better knowing they were somewhere safe."

"Of course," Jake answers.

Taylor looks at Eagle and nods. "Everyone that knows what you're doing, head out. Shelby, you stay and talk to Eagle. He knows what he's doing."

In just minutes the building is cleared out of everyone except myself, Eagle and his crew.

"Come on Mama Bear, let's sit down and figure out the next move." Eagle gently takes my arm and leads me to the couch.

The whole time I was freaking out my kids were my only focus but now that I can relax it's like my systems are kicking back in. The moment I sit down, I jump back up "Get out of my way" I yell as I dash for the bathroom to vomit.

I would laugh at how fast they move aside if my body wasn't trying to expel my internal organs.

After exercising the contents of my stomach I feel weak and shaky. Thank goodness Mac is standing outside the bathroom door waiting to help me. Looking around I see all the other guys standing as far as they can get from me.

"Mac, why are they acting like that?" I whisper.

He laughs, "Weak stomachs, the bunch o' them. Listening to ye, turning yer insides out had em all gagging."

Taking another look around, I do see a few green faces. These big bikers queasy at a bit of vomit, has me laughing.

Letting me lean on him for support, as we go back to the couch, Mac leans down and whispers so only I can hear him, "When's the wee one due?"

Instead of answering him, I shake my head and change the subject. "Is it true you don't wear anything under your kilt even when you're riding?"

"Aye, mostly. I do scootch into some short pants when we'll be riding a long distance. Don't feel ta good when me balls stick ta leather."

Eagle steps over and smacks Mac on the back of the head, "Glitch's woman doesn't need to know about how often you gotta peel your balls off your bike seat."

"Remind me to never ride his bike," I giggle taking a seat.

As soon as I'm seated, Sticks hands me a bottle of water. "Thank you," I tell him.

Once again the guys are talking around me, instead of to me. I sit back and listen as Eagle plans how they are going to take down Greyson.

I check my phone and realize Glitch has been gone for a really long time. That's when it becomes clear to me these guys are planning to go in guns blazing, but it's a park for goodness sake and people could get hurt.

Excusing myself from the room, I inform the guys that I need to run up to my apartment for something. Mac offers to come with me but I assure him I can handle going upstairs by myself.

Once I'm out of the building, I pull out my cell phone and arrange for a ride share to pick me up at the end of the block. In my apartment, I dive deep into my closet to dig out the safe I keep there.

It's a small safe, just big enough to hold my important documents and my gun. The gun is what I pull out before locking it back up.

Once I have it hidden under my jacket. I slip back out and run behind Poison Pen, then between a few buildings, and out at the end of the block where a car is waiting for me.

Chapter 11

Greyson

Where is that bitch! Does she think I'm going to stand around all day? I gave her simple instructions. Meet me at Kincaid Park!

Instead, her fucking biker cunt shows up! I hope she enjoyed riding his cock while she had the chance because I'm not letting him live to use it ever again.

Of course, I don't plan on her living past today anyways.

Maybe I'll bury them together, that would be poetic. The cheating whore and the biker bitch in the same hole.

Dumbass thought he could sneak up on me, but I've been hiding out here for the last month. I know every nook and cranny in this park.

Laughed like a hyena while I tasered his ass and yelled "Timber" as he fell. Funniest thing I ever saw. He didn't think it was funny, nope. He jerked and twitched as I tied him to a tree.

I wonder, if I turn the taser all the way up, will he piss his pants? That would be fucking hilarious!

When the cheating whore gets here, I'll let her watch him piss himself then see if she still wants to spread her legs for this pussy.

"Where the fuck is she!" I shout. The sound of my voice echoes through the trees.

"Your note said the park." My prisoner pipes up, but I didn't ask him.

"I told her to meet me at Kincaid Park!" I snap back as I send 20,000 volts through him.

"But," he gasps for breath. "This park covers over 100 acres of land. How the fuck is she supposed to know what part of the park you're waiting in?"

Dammit! I ditched my phone so I couldn't be traced. This cuntnugget has a point. "You got a phone on you?" I angrily ask him.

"In my pocket," he answers.

I check his bindings before I retrieve the phone from his pocket.

I'm not fucking stupid but he is. Doesn't even have a lock screen on his phone.

Scrolling through his contacts I don't see her name. "What is she listed under?" I question him as I set off the taser once more.

Gasping for breath, he shouts, "Angel, she's listed as Angel. The first contact on my phone."

That sets me off, laughing again. "Angel, Ha! That cheating whore is no angel! She's a fucking succubus, sucking the life out of a man. She's not even a good succubus, just lays there while I rut into her. At least the pussy is tight, right?"

My words are pissing him off but there's not a damn thing he can do about it. I wish she was here to see how impudent her biker bitch is.

Hitting the call button, I wait for her to answer.

"Glitch where are you?" She questions.

"Not your little biker boy, wife. Where are you?" I snap at her.

"I'm about five minutes away, Greyson. Please don't hurt him." She begs.

"Take the side entrance then follow the hiking trail that leads to Lookout point." I instruct her.

I hear her talk to someone, but I can't make out the words she must have her hand over the microphone.

"Who are you talking to? I told you to come alone!" I growl out.

"I'm alone Greyson, I swear. I don't have a car so I had to call a ride-share. The driver is going to drop me off and leave, that's all." She stammers out.

"If you're lying to me I'm going to drop your little bastard son out of the plane over the ocean, Bitch." I respond.

"I promise Grey, I'm alone." I don't wait to hear anymore, disconnecting the call while she's still talking.

Throwing the cell phone on the ground, I find great pleasure in stomping it to little bits.

"Why do you hate your son so much?" Biker bitch asks me out of the blue.

"Boys turn into men and men take everything from their fathers. I worked my ass off, put up with whiney bitches like you and I'm not about to let that bastard take everything from me." he looks confused by my answer.

"But fathers are supposed to raise their sons to take over one day. A real father would teach his son to be a man, not plot to kill him." He tells me.

"My father was a weak, useless man! The day I put him down he cursed me. That fucker looked me in the eyes as he took his last breath and swore any son of mine would take vengeance for him. I intend to end him before that can happen!"

Shelby

The driver left me at the park entrance and peeled out of here like his ass was on fire. Thankfully the trail Grey told me to take isn't very far.

As I look around, I wonder what he's thinking. This park doesn't seem as well used as the one I normally take the kids to, but there are people around.

When I took the kids to Stella's there were a few snowflakes falling but it has steadily gotten worse since then.

I can only see about twenty feet in front of me, which is bad because it means I won't know when I get to wherever Grey is. But, it's also good because it means I can sneak up on him.

As I follow the trail I think back over our marriage trying to recall any signs of the man my ex-husband is today.

His father passed away a couple of years before I met him and his mother died when he was a child. So I never met any of his family.

He worked for my Dad for a few years but didn't show any sign he wanted to date me until right before my parents left on the vacation that killed them. He made me feel special with fancy dinners and movie premieres.

I understand his disappointment when Bryson was born because he wanted a little girl so badly.

It had been the only thing he talked about my whole pregnancy. I just never imagined his feelings were so deep that he actually wants to kill his own son.

Getting pregnant with Dyna wasn't planned but when I found I was having a girl, I thought maybe Greyson would go back to being the man he used to be. The one that I fell in love with.

Now that I've been with Glitch, I realize maybe I never loved Grey. Maybe I just needed someone to remind me I was still alive and not buried with my parents.

I regret staying married as long as I did but I don't regret any of the time I spent with him. It gave me my kids and they are precious.

As far as I know Grey has no idea that the kids are safe so I don't plan on telling him. If I don't walk out of these woods, he won't get his hands on them.

I made sure Taylor has the papers filed regarding custody of Bryson and Dyna if anything happens to me.

There is a bend in the trail ahead and I hear a voice in the distance. The map at the trail head showed it looping back, so this must be where Greyson is waiting for me.

I step off the trail and slip between the trees, creeping closer. The closer I get, the clearer I recognize it as being Greyson.

The revelation that he killed his own father, knocks me for a loop. It's like I never knew Greyson Porter at all.

Taking advantage of all the noise Grey is making I move around in between the trees, trying to figure out where Glitch is.

I've made almost a full circle when I finally spot him tied to a tree.

First I consider getting behind him and cutting him loose but as agitated as Grey is, I don't think I can remain hidden much longer.

I know that Glitch has a knife in his boot but he probably can't reach it the way Grey has him tied up.

I creep up behind Glitch and carefully pull the knife from his boot. He doesn't even know I'm there until I put the knife in his hand.

Giving him a squeeze, I slip back into the woods and around to where the trail is just out of view.

Greyson yells, "Where the fuck is she?" just before I step back onto the trail.

"I'm here, Grey," I call out as I move closer.

"What took you so long?" he asks.

"I had to make arrangements for my job. I couldn't just not be there to watch the kids." I try to calm him.

"I don't have all day!" He shouts.

"Grey, I'm here. You need to let Adam go. There are people looking for him." It's the first time I've used Glitch's real name. I'm hoping he takes the hint and gets out of here.

He throws his head back and laughs, "Neither one of you is walking out of here! You took my precious away from me and spread your legs for him! What does he have that I don't? I gave you a house and took care of everything you and that little brat could ever want. What can he give you?"

Instead of answering, I ask him, "What are you going to do? Kill us and leave our bodies here on the trail? The police will catch you before you even leave the park."

"Look around you Greyson." Glitch says. "It's the first snow of the season. You won't be able to go anywhere. Flights will be canceled and roads will be shut down."

"I know what you're doing!" Greyson growls yanking on his hair. He has some kind of weapon in his right hand but I can't see what it is clearly. "You think I'm going to let you live so I can get away. It won't work! I need you to die, once you're dead, I can get control of your trust fund!"

"Greyson, I will sign over my trust fund right now, if it means I'll never have to see you again." I tell him.

"I'M NOT STUPID! You can't sign shit over until you turn thirty!" He shouts at me then turns and charges towards Glitch with his weapon raised.

I don't pause to think about what I'm about to do, I pull out my gun and fire. Greyson turns back to me as if confused. "What have you done?" Grey stutters as he falls to his knees.

I'm stunned, I can't believe I shot him. When someone's arms wrap around my shoulders, I blink and Glitch is holding me. How did he get over here? He was tied to a tree. I look at the tree and the ropes are laying around the trunk.

Glitch is talking to me but the words evaporate before they reach my ears. The snowflakes are so pretty, falling and turning red once they reach the ground.

I watch, mesmerized by the spreading pool of blood under Greyson's body.

"I think she's in shock," a voice finally breaks through to me.

"Get her back to her kids. She'll be fine once she sees they are safe." I look up and see Eagle talking.

"My kids! Where are my kids?" I manage to say.

"Everyone is waiting for you at Taylor's house. Arin wanted the kids somewhere safe." Eagle says.

"Glitch," I whisper his name. "Take me to my babies, please."

Chapter 12

Shelby

I round the corner of Arin and Taylor's house, finding the kids playing in the snow. My heart pounds in my chest and tears stream down my face as the realization hits me that they are truly safe.

Taylor finally notices me standing there and gets the kids attention, pointing to where I am.

"Dyna! Bryson!" I yell out, my voice choked with all the emotion of the past few hours.

Their little faces light up with huge smiles as they race towards me. Hitting me straight in the legs.

"Mommy!" They both jump up and down.

Bending down, I take them both into my arms, holding them tightly to me.

"Are you okay?" I ask, my question more directed towards my sweet little boy.

"Uh, huh." They both speak at the same time.

Letting them go, Dyna runs back off to play. Like any other small child, never knowing how much danger she truly was in.

"Where's daddy?" Bryson asks, looking behind me and I remember that Glitch is there.

I watch as Glitch bends down, putting a hand on Bry's shoulder.

"You don't have to worry about that any more son. I promise you, no one will ever take you away from your mom again." He says and I watch as my sweet little boy wraps his arms around Glitch, not letting go for several long minutes.

Setting him back onto his own feet, he smiles up at Glitch with a smile that seems to light up the entire world.

"Guess I'll go help the girls build a castle." Bry groans as if it's a task that would surely kill him and I hide a smile behind my hand.

"Good man. You go help the girls." Glitch tells him just as he runs off in that direction.

Watching the kids play, my heart is completely full. Sure there would be hurdles down the road. Bryson may even benefit from going to therapy after all the trauma he's endured in his short little life.

There's just one thing left though. I think as I look back over at Glitch.

"We need to talk." I say to him.

He holds up his hand to stop me. "Look, Babe, I already know I owe you an apology for being a major asshole lately and I am sorry for that. But..."

"But?" I laugh.

"But I will not ever apologize for doing what I think is the right thing to keep you safe. To keep you all safe." He says and my heart softens even more for this man.

"Well, thank you for the apology." I lean over kissing his cheek. "But that's not what I wanted to talk about."

"Wait. You can't break it off with me, woman! I fucking love you!" His face goes red like it does when he's gearing up for an argument.

"Good. Cause I love you too but..."

"But? No, there's no 'but'. You, me and the kids. That is all!" He says, crossing his arms.

"Are you going to let me finish or continue with your brand of crazy?" I demand, crossing my own arms.

His face registers surprise at first then he begins laughing.

"Please, sweetheart, continue." He rolls his eyes and my own narrows at him.

"Do you mean it? Me, you and the kids?" I ask.

"Hell yes, I mean it. I know I didn't help to make them but they mean just as much to me as you do." He looks at me like I've lost my mind.

"And if there is one that you helped to create?" My heart slams in my chest as I watch his eyes widen.

"You mean...we...we're going to have a baby?" He almost whispers and I shake my head yes, unable to speak.

"Fuck, yeah!" He exclaims, grabbing me and twirling me around in a circle.

"What's going on?" Arin demands, looking at us both as she and all the rest of the crew walk outside.

"We're having a baby!" He exclaims but then his face goes serious. "Oh fuck, I'm going to be a dad. Oh, shit." He sits down hard on the snow.

Arin and Mika start laughing as all the guys come over to pat him on the back.

"No worries man, you'll be great!" Atka laughs as well.

I shake my head as I watch all the commotion playing out in front of me. I really do love these people. I was scared to death when we first moved here but not now. Now I really have a family.

A family that would do anything for me and mine. A family that I would protect at all costs, even at the price of my own life.

Glitch

The last few months have been the best weeks of my entire life. The girls from Poison Pen have been helping Shelby to plan our wedding.

It took several weeks for me to convince her to marry me. The woman is just as damn hard headed as the rest of them. It took Bryson helping to plead my case to close the deal.

That little man is my best friend and I've told him so. He goes almost everywhere with me these days. We did get him into therapy though to help him to work out any feelings he was having over his biological father.

Shelby is starting to show in her pregnancy but she's not let her slow her down any.

She decided only a week ago that she wanted to learn how to tattoo. It turns out that my woman is one hell of an artist. She's already informed me though that I can't get any freebies.

We moved in together right after Greyson was shot. The cops did a quick investigation of the entire situation but closed the case pretty quickly.

Thank fuck for that! Eagle was a little worried about them digging too far into the club and its members. We're not all on the up and up.

Speaking of, I watch as Spector walks quickly through the clubhouse, headed for the door.

"Wonder why he's in a hurry?" Mac says from behind the bar.

"I heard that he had another job overseas." Sticks pipes up.

Mac and I turn to look at Sticks with shock.

"You really need to stop over-hearing what isn't meant for your ears!" I tell him in a growl.

"Well people need to stop talking so fucking loud!" He growls back, jumping up to stomp away.

"Dat boy will na ever learn. He's na even a full patched member yet." Mac shakes his head.

"He'll be fine. And why isn't he? He's been here since he was a kid. Doesn't seem like he's ever going anywhere. He knows almost everything about the club. Why hasn't Eagle patched him in yet?" I wonder out loud.

"Spector. Dat be why fer ya." Mac whispers before walking away.

He's most likely right although I still don't understand why Spector would stand in the way. Leaving it for another day to contemplate, I wave goodbye to Mac as I head out.

It's time to go home to my woman and kids. That thought alone, keeps a smile on my face all the way to my front door.

THE END

Coming soon from Rae Goldman
<u>https://books2read.com/ThornebayLucas</u>
Lucas
April 2023

Lucas

When a plane crashes on Prince of Wales Island in remote Alaska, the only people with the equipment to get in and out of the area are the Thorne Bay Logging crew. As the team Medic it is Lucas' responsibility to make sure everyone gets in and out alive, including the woman they are sent to rescue.

Megan

Testify against the Mob, they said. We'll protect you, they said. Nobody would ever think to look for you in Alaska, they said. But nobody predicted the plane crash that splattered my picture all over the media. The plane crash that killed me. I must be dead because Polar bears don't turn into hot red headed lumberjacks in real life.

Available now from Rae Goldman
Elaina's Hope

https://books2read.com/Millermafia

Elaina always knew her Father had her life planned for her and there was no escape. However when she overhears his plans to sell her into forced marriage with a man old enough to be her Grandfather, she takes her fate into her own hands. Only everyone else seems to be a step ahead of her.

Grant unknowingly gets roped into Elaina's scheme and does everything he can to help her escape but is it going to be enough to save her?

Jeramiah's Possession

The Company Series

*J*eramiah

My life is a solitary one lived on the fringes of society. Blending in but staying in the shadows. Friends are few, if you can even call them friends. All of us, working for The Company. All of us, more deadly than the world around us knows.

My new mission was a simple one. Gather intel and get out. I had every intention of doing just that until I locked eyes with her.

Milena

Recently losing the only person in this world who cared about me was rough but nowhere near what I'm currently going through.

Hopefully, I can get out of here alive and make my stepfather pay for what he's done.

GET IT HERE: **https://books2read.com/ JeramiahsPossession**

Elven Oath

The Dragon Clan has been at war with the Elves for centuries. Neither side is willing to give up the old feud regardless of no one remembering what started it.

There's a new war brewing on the horizon. An enemy that is looking to destroy every Dragon shifter and Elf alike.

A marriage between the two clans will ensure that both sides fight beside each other.

That's if Prince Aodhan and Princess Vevina don't kill each other first.

Can the Prince and Princess put aside their differences to save both their clans?

GET IT HERE: https://books2read.com/ElvenOath

Apple Martinis

Sweet Cocktails Series Book 1

Piper
Life has sucked for me recently. My mom passed away and then I caught my boyfriend "working overtime" in our bedroom with his secretary when I came home early from work.

When my friends suggested a little vacation to the beach, I packed up my bags and drove straight down to the Flora-Bama line without making any reservations.

Everything was going amazingly well until life decided to suck yet again. Now I'm tied up with a bunch of other women inside some kind of shipping crate with no hope that anyone will save me.

Rome
Leaving my family behind years ago for a different kind of life, I've done well for myself, making my own way working as a bartender for the exclusive Sweet Cocktails franchise.

Meeting Piper should have been like any other meeting I've had with women here. Instead, I like her immediately. Spending time with her, I can't wait for more. Then one night someone grabs her from the street before I can get there.

I was prepared to never lay eyes on my twin brothers again until I need their help. I just hope they don't turn me away or worse...

Shoot me in the head.

GET IT HERE: https://www.amazon.com/dp/B0C6HS8CHY

More from Author Marissa Ann

Marissa Ann spends her time in rural North Mississippi with her husband, the kids and all of their animals on a hobby farm.

She always said she would write books one day even though many thought she never would. She made a promise to a childhood friend who left this world for the next in 2015. That she would finally write and publish at least one.

Her first book hit the market in 2018 and she's never looked back. She now has several out with many more scheduled for release. Want to stay up to date with new releases, giveaways and all the cool things?

Join Marissa Online and Sign Up For Her Newsletter

Website: https://www.authormarissaann.com/
OR JOIN **Marissa Ann Romance Readers** on Facebook.

Did you love *Shelby's Secret*? Then you should read *Snake's Fate*[1] by Marissa Ann!

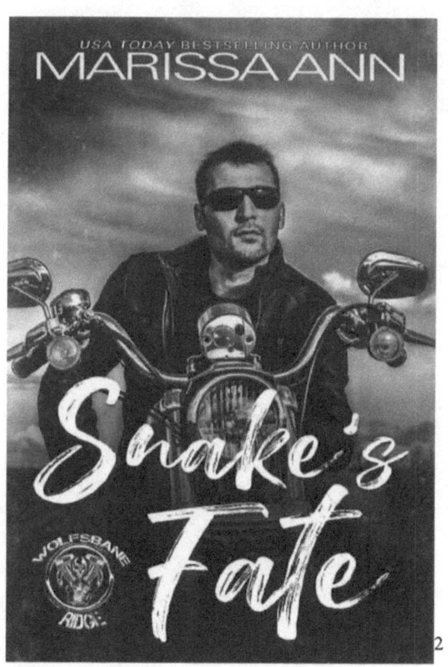

[2]

Snake

Computers and Harley's are forever. Women are for one night. That's how I've lived my life for the past twelve years, never letting anyone in.

My life has been amazing inside the Wolfsbane MC. These men are more than friends, they are my brothers. Everything in life was going great...until she showed up again with bad news and a secret that rocks me to my core.

Andi

---

1. https://books2read.com/u/bxrPQv

2. https://books2read.com/u/bxrPQv

I knew it would be hard for him to find out this way. He disappeared from town almost twelve years ago without even a note, I wasn't expecting to run into him again after all these years.

His eyes are now filled with anger. I just don't know if it's directed at me or the circumstances that got us to this point. I should have made different choices back then. We all should have.

Also by Marissa Ann

Night Howler's MC
Reaper's Jewels
Grease

Night Howler's MC New Orleans
Buzz
Skeeter

Poison Pen
Baratta's Darkness
Lily's Shadow
Arin's Light
Mika's Heart
Cass' Vow
Shelby's Secret

The Company
Giovanni's Obsession
Jeramiah's Possession

Three King's Ridge
King's Heart

Wolfsbane Ridge MC
Timber's Fairy
Blade's Pixie
Blood's Angel
Wrench's Salvation
Bear's Saviour
Torque's Gaze
Fang's Miracle
Snake's Fate

Standalone
Sea's Of Rissa
All I've Got
Elven Oath

Also by Rae Goldman

Poison Pen
Baratta's Darkness
Lily's Shadow
Arin's Light
Mika's Heart
Cass' Vow
Shelby's Secret

www.ingramcontent.com/pod-product-compliance
Lightning Source LLC
Chambersburg PA
CBHW061429160726
47995CB00003B/812